ASK ANYBODY

OTHER YEARLING BOOKS YOU WILL ENJOY:

A GIRL CALLED AL, *Constance C. Greene*
I KNOW YOU, AL, *Constance C. Greene*
YOUR OLD PAL, AL, *Constance C. Greene*
AL(EXANDRA) THE GREAT, *Constance C. Greene*
DOTTY'S SUITCASE, *Constance C. Greene*
DOUBLE DARE O'TOOLE, *Constance C. Greene*
I AND SPROGGY, *Constance C. Greene*
RAMONA QUIMBY, AGE 8, *Beverly Cleary*
RAMONA AND HER MOTHER, *Beverly Cleary*
RAMONA AND HER FATHER, *Beverly Cleary*

YEARLING BOOKS are designed especially to entertain and enlighten young people. Charles F. Reasoner, Professor Emeritus of Children's Literature and Reading, New York University, is consultant to this series.

For a complete listing of all Yearling titles, write to Dell Publishing Co., Inc., Promotion Department, P.O. Box 3000, Pine Brook, N.J. 07058.

To my Maine friends,
each and every one of them

1

Schuyler Sweet is anything but. Ask anybody. I ought to know. I am Schuyler Sweet. I'm halfway to twelve, a bad age in a woman. Or in anybody else, for that matter. Sometimes I don't have the sweetest disposition in the world. My mother was like me when she was my age. She told me so herself. But now she's got herself sorted out and she's as sweet as pie. When it behooves her. Right now it's behooving her because she's in love again. She said after the divorce she would never fall in love again as it makes a woman too vulnerable. My father said he had never noticed she had a vulnerable bone in her body. But that was, as I said, right after my mother and father got divorced and they were not themselves. People always say that as if being yourself were a good thing. In my opinion, it depends. Some yourselfs I could mention are very turdy and disagreeable people. In their case, it would be better if they were someone else. In many cases, if you're not yourself, it's an improvement. If you get my meaning.

Take me. Sometimes when I'm myself, I can be very nasty. When I'm not myself, some might think I was a darling girl. I'm not myself very seldom, so my reputation, generally speaking, is not so hot. I don't know why. I like people. Most people. Well, a lot of people. Some people. I don't like people who are slobs, though, or people who are greedy or stuck-up or conceited. Or stingy. Or phony. I guess I hate phonies more than anybody.

As I said, I can be mean. It just pops out, the meanness. Every time I tell myself I've been mean for the last time, something happens and—presto—I find myself being mean all over again. Once I stuck a rusty needle under my fingernail so I would be reminded not to be mean if I felt a fit of meanness coming on. All that happened was that I got an infection and had to have a tetanus shot, which is no picnic.

I was trying to mortify my flesh, as the saints did in

2

days of yore. No wonder so many saints keeled over in droves back then. They didn't have tetanus shots or any of the advantages of modern medicine in case they too stuck rusty needles under their skin. I think it must be easier to be a saint these days than it was in olden times. However, saints seem to have lost status and no longer occupy a place of honor in our society. A sad state of affairs.

My feet are growing while the rest of me stands still, canceling my immediate plans to be a ballet dancer. Perhaps the rest of me will catch up with my feet in due course, but at the moment it seems unlikely. My best friend, Rowena Hastings, says I remind her of a bull in a china shop. There are plenty of things she reminds me of, but I refrain from mentioning them because at the moment I'm on a kindly kick. It's very odd. Every time I go on a kindly kick someone says something cruel to me and it's a struggle to stay kindly. Rowena, I might add, is developing into the type that has boys writing notes and stuffing them down the back of her sweater or shirt when she's not looking. The notes say clever things like "U R 4 ME" or "Meet you at the Laundromat. Bring suds." It's not what they say, it's the way they say it, I always say.

My mother is a photographer. She specializes in pictures of wild animals. Next week she's going to Africa to shoot a layout of a famous game reserve for a magazine. The four of us—my father, my brothers, and I—will keep house. My father is an artist, a cartoonist, really. He does the comic strip "Plotsie," which is about a kid who can't do anything right. Plotsie's been quite a success, so a lot of people must relate to him. My father works at home, one reason he and my mother got a divorce. They suffered from too much togetherness. That's what they said. They had fifteen years of togetherness, and it finally got to them. I can understand that. Most fathers go off to work in the morning and arrive home in time for supper, full of jolly little tales and bits of funny dialogue they've picked up along the way, which they can relate to their wives and children to liven up their day. Not my father. He sits around scratching his head and grousing about how he can't get a good line for Plotsie's next adventure. Cartoonists, by and large, are somewhat eccentric.

We live in Maine in a village that calls itself the prettiest village in the entire state. It even has a sign posted to that effect on the outskirts of town so tourists will see it and write lots of postcards back home to prove they've been to the prettiest village in Maine. Who decides which is the prettiest village, anyway? Do they take a vote? Or does the mayor or some politician say, "This is the prettiest village in the state"? My father says it's the Chamber of Commerce. He's probably right.

I don't think anyone can decide what's the prettiest

4

or best or worst of anything. All the citizens should have a vote to see what's the prettiest, ugliest, smelliest. Whatever. As far as I'm concerned, too much importance is put on looks. It's a known fact, however, that pretty gets you further in life than ugly. Ask anybody. Good-looking people have it all over the uglies of this world. They get to play the lead in the school play, sing solos in the glee club even if their voices are mediocre. And they also get to be on the school traffic squad, which means they boss everybody and act like little Hitlers just because they wear arm bands. They shout, "Slow down or I'll report you!" as if they were actual arms of the law. I've noticed when perfectly ordinary people get on the traffic squad, they change overnight. Sort of like Dr. Jekyll and Mr. Hyde. If you get my meaning.

If you think from reading the above that I'm not one of the world's good lookers, you're right. My face wouldn't stop a clock. Neither would it launch a thousand ships. I look like my mother. The boys look like my father, who is handsome in an offbeat way. He has a Yankee face, long and lean and rugged. My mother is small, but her posture is excellent so people think she's a lot taller. She's nice looking in a folksy, midwestern way. People are always surprised to learn she's quite famous in her field. She's even been on television. Everybody in town tuned in. Rowena said, "Your mother seemed very nervous." That's all she said. Not, "Your mother certainly was good," or, "I thought your mother spoke very clearly." Just, "Your mother seemed very nervous."

Rowena's mother is a housewife. She told someone she didn't think it was right for Mary Sweet to be running around the world taking pictures of rhinos and hippos when she should be home checking her husband and children for boils. That's what she said: boils. The Hastings kids have piles of boils. Which is better than piles of piles any day in the week. Piles are gross things that attack your rear end. Their proper name is "hemorrhoids," which should give you some idea. My father had them once. After that he rigged up a contraption he could lean against while he worked instead of sitting down eight hours a day at his drawing board. He told me people who got piles usually sat down for a large part of the day.

I don't know how I got into this. I certainly didn't intend to discuss hemorrhoids.

One more thing. Some say that boils are due to a vitamin deficiency in the diet. Have I ever hinted at this to Rowena? Never.

2

My brother Stanley is seven and my brother Sidney is five. We call Stanley Tad, short for tadpole, which is a baby frog. My father said that's what Tad looked like when he was born—a baby frog. Sidney is called Sidney because it suits him. Sidney is small for his age but, as I say, he's only five. He's got lots of time. I'm named for my father, who is also Schuyler Sweet. What happened was this:

I was the first kid in the family. When I was born, my father took a long, hard look at me and said, "That's it, Mary. No more." First-time parents have difficulty adjusting to the fact that new babies are frequently repulsive. My father told me that, so I know it's so. My mother, however, said I was darling. "No matter what your father says, you were a darling baby," she told me. My grandfather came all the way from Indiana to check out me, his first grandchild. He leaned over the crib, stared down at me for a minute, then said, "Feed it and water it and it'll turn out fine." Then he handed over a check for fifty dollars to take care of my college education, and went back to Indiana to tend his cows.

But, human beings what they are, after a respite Tad came along life's highway. Then, in two more years, Sidney showed up. Sidney was the pick of the litter, with big blue eyes and enough hair for three babies. I don't know why they gave us all names beginning with S. People sometimes have a hard time keeping our names straight. Sometimes the boys and I sit around saying all our names as fast as we can. We sound like a bunch of snakes at a slumber party, all those *sssssssssss* sounds. Only my mother, whose name is Mary, as I think I mentioned, lacks an S. And soon, if she marries this man she thinks she loves, she won't even be Sweet any more. I think she'll be sorry, but she says he's the man for her. She said this in front of my father in a loud voice. He only scratched his head and thought about Plotsie.

We live in a Maine-type farmhouse. It's one room deep but stretches out along the top of Blueberry Hill, which is the hill we live on. My mother sleeps in one end in her studio, my father sleeps in the other in his studio, and me and the boys sleep in the middle. It works all right. For the time being.

Tad lost his first tooth last week, and he put it under his pillow so the tooth fairy would come get it and leave him a quarter. He wrapped it up good and tight inside a grubby piece of paper, folding it this way and that so the tooth would fit tight and not get lost. He counted on that quarter. He had about a hundred plans for that quarter. He was proud of losing his first tooth too, because that meant he was on his way to old age. In the middle of the night Sidney got out of bed and stole Tad's tooth and flushed it down the toilet. We only found out about it next morning when Tad let out a roar of rage when he looked under his pillow and saw there was nothing there. Sidney never lies. He doesn't know how. So when Tad went tearing around the house shouting, "Somebody stole my tooth! Who stole my tooth? Who stole it?" Sidney piped up and said, "I did."

That took courage. If you could've seen Tad's face, you'd know what I mean. Tad's big and strong for his age. But Sidney just stood his ground with his feet planted wide and a fierce look on his white face. His face was so white I thought he was going to keel over.

He was scared but he stayed put, and Tad came at him with his fists clenched, ready to punch the stuffing out of him. My father held on to Tad so he couldn't do Sidney any damage.

"Why'd you do that?" Tad shouted over and over. "Why'd you steal my tooth? You're jealous, that's why. You're too little to lose a tooth. You're jealous!" All the while he was flailing his arms, trying to get loose from my father's grip so he could pound Sidney's head into the rug.

At last, tears streaming down his face, Sidney said, "I didn't want that old tooth fairy coming into my room. I didn't want any old tooth fairy sneaking in while I was asleep and reaching under the pillow. I'm scared of the tooth fairy. I didn't want him coming in while I wasn't looking." Sidney always calls the tooth fairy Him. I don't know why.

Everybody knows it's a Her.

Poor little Sidney. He doesn't like to know about fairies or leprechauns. He imagines little men moving stealthily around the house, darting from tree to tree like Indians on the warpath, ready to shoot their arrows through the windows and maybe through his head. He looks in the closet, too, before he goes to bed, to make sure there's no one there. He also checks under his bed. And, if you want to be really mean, hide in the dark at the top of the stairs and pounce out at him. That scares him silly.

Dad says he'll grow out of it. In the meantime he's a gentle little boy. I wish he'd get tougher, for his sake. But if he did, he wouldn't be Sidney.

Dad gave Tad a quarter to make up for the stolen tooth. But Tad said it wasn't the same thing, although I notice he didn't give the quarter back. But I know what he means. The night after it happened, I read a story to Sidney before his bedtime. Tad's nose was still out of joint. He said he didn't want to hear any old story so it was just me and Sidney. Halfway through the story, Sidney put his thumb in his mouth and made little sucking noises. He hadn't sucked his thumb in weeks.

"I can't help it," he told me. "I'm sorry I did what I did. But tonight I need my thumb. It comforts me."

I'm glad my mother and father didn't give up after they had me.

3

Rowena Hastings says I've been getting very prickly of late. She says I never used to be prickly but now I am. I don't think she's right. If she doesn't quit saying things like that, Rowena and I may no longer be best friends. Rowena has beautiful long brown hair, which she rinses in vinegar to bring out its red highlights. She uses about a quart of vinegar a month. Whenever the strong scent of vinegar is in the air, you may be sure Rowena is in the neighborhood.

I have a second-best friend whose name is Betty

Binns. Betty's mother sells cosmetics from door to door. She's a large woman with a wide, smooth face and dark hair, which she scrapes back and ties with a rubber band or a bit of yarn. Some have been known to pull their shades and hide in the closet when Betty's mother approaches, as she's famous for not taking no for an answer. Betty takes after her mother, in both looks and temperament. Betty's father is a TV repairman. Their garage is chock-full of broken-down TV sets. Betty's father has the reputation of being slow but sure. Boys don't stuff notes down Betty's shirt any more than they do mine. Betty is very intelligent. She reads best-sellers. Only best-sellers. Then she tells you the plot. Betty can get quite boring when she tells the plots of all the books she reads, but so far I haven't told her she's boring. I think that would be mean. Even for me.

Have you ever heard anyone say, "When you come right down to it, I'm a pretty boring person"? I bet you haven't. Nobody thinks of themselves as a boring person. Ask anybody. Say, "Do you think you're a boring person?" and they'll probably look very surprised and say, "Well, now that you mention it, no, not really." Most people think they're fairly interesting. Not outrageously interesting, just moderately so. Very few people actually say to themselves, Boy, am I ever a bore! It goes against the grain, so to speak.

I'm a fairly interesting person. Not always but sometimes. I try to ask intelligent questions and be interested in other people. Like I always find out how many brothers and sisters kids have and what their favorite food is and what television programs they watch. Where their mothers and fathers were born and all. I took a magazine quiz last week to find out how interesting I really am. I scored between seventy-five and eighty, which means I'm fairly interesting. I'd like to raise my score so that I'm classified as a Very Interesting Person rather than just a Fairly. Which is why I'm making an effort to listen intently and ask good questions instead of talking about myself all the time. I won't mention the names of some people who are guilty of talking about themselves. Their initials, however, are R. H. and, sometimes, B. B.

I think it's good to be curious. I don't mean nosy, I mean curious. I like to know about people: where they come from, what they do for a living, what they think about. How old they are. Once a friend of my mother's came over and we were chatting and she said to me, "How old are you?" So I told her. Then I said, "How old are *you*?" back to her. She froze. I mean, I could feel her freezing right in front of me. Her face got very cold, and she left soon afterward without telling me how old she was. When I told my mother, she fell on the floor, laughing.

"Even her own mother doesn't know how old she is!"

my mother howled, tears streaming down her face, she was laughing so hard.

Betty Binns just founded the Chum Club. She sent out notices saying membership dues were ten cents a month. Each member, Betty said, had to have a yard sale in her yard. All members of the Chum Club would contribute items to be sold. Proceeds would go to various charitable institutions. Betty sat by her telephone, picking her cuticle, waiting for her phone to ring. She received a blow to her solar plexus, never mind her pride, when no one called. Not a single person. So then she got on the horn and asked everyone in her famous huffy voice why they were sitting on their hands and not calling her.

"I thought perhaps you were out of town," she said. If any of us goes as far as Bangor once a year, it's a big deal. "Maybe your father forgot to pay his phone bill," was another thing she said, earning her no friends and a few enemies. No one wanted to join her Chum Club, it seemed.

"Such a dumb name for a club," Rowena hissed. "I never heard of such a dumb name for a club." Still, if Rowena hadn't received an invitation, rest assured the fur would've flown. We said if we were expected to contribute items to the yard sale, and go to the trouble of lettering signs and tacking them up on the school bulletin board and putting them in the window of the gen-

15

eral store and outside the post office and all, and hanging signs on trees giving directions on how to get there, we wanted the proceeds for ourselves.

Some hard feelings resulted. Betty said she felt sorry for people who were so grasping. But, after a little thought, like about three minutes, she called us up and said O.K., scratch the charitable contributions. Three people signed up for Betty's Chum Club. Me and her and Rowena. Then things came to a grinding halt. Our membership roster fell on its face. I suggested Sidney and Tad as back-up members. After making considerable derogatory remarks as to the suitability of accepting boys, Betty and Rowena finally agreed. But when I mentioned the Chum Club to the boys, they made vomit noises and ran and hid. So for the time being it'll be just the three of us. If you ask me, three members aren't enough for a club. But that's where it stands now. Our first yard sale is scheduled to be the last weekend in April. If it's not snowing. In Maine you never know. Our snow date is the first weekend in May, to be on the safe side. We want to beat the mayflies. They arrive later on in May. No one is safe from them. They have a ferocious bite that lasts for days and raises huge welts.

My mother gave me a couple of ashtrays for the sale. She and my father both quit smoking, so they have all these ashtrays nobody uses. One says, "Old doctors never die, they just lose their patients." That's my favorite.

I went through my jewelry box and chose a necklace I found last year in the movies. It was tucked down in my seat and I thought at first it might be real diamonds. It turned out not to be real anything. Rowena said her mother said we could have her old fur coat. We got all excited and raced over to have a look. After we inspected Rowena's mother's coat, we decided to put a price of two dollars on it, so as to leave room for bargaining. People who go to yard sales expect to bargain. It's no fun if something is marked $1.50 and you pay $1.50 and that's that. Bargaining's half the fun. So you should price items accordingly. I learned that from an article I read in a magazine telling you how to go about organizing a yard sale.

I smell a fight coming up with Betty. So far, she hasn't contributed anything. She claims the Chum Club was her idea so she thinks that should let her off the hook and that she doesn't have to contribute anything. Rowena and I are furious.

I think there's more than meets the eye with a yard sale. It looks as if some personality conflicts were cropping up. Tact may be required to resolve these conflicts. I think we should take a vote on who has the most tact and let that person handle the matter.

One thing sure, it won't be Rowena.

4

We're in luck. A new family moved into the house on the end of our road yesterday. There are a lot of kids, Rowena's mother says. Five or six, maybe. Rowena's mother usually knows. When she isn't being a housewife, she scours the surrounding countryside looking for newcomers. She has appointed herself the official newcomer welcomer. When she sights the moving van on the outskirts of town, Rowena's mother hotfoots it for home and gets all doozied up in her print dress and her black shoes with heels and stuffs a scented hanky down her bosom and marches out with a loaf of her freshly baked bread tucked under her arm to welcome the newcomers. There can never be enough newcomers for her, she says.

My father says that bread is enough to head them off at the pass. He says if the newcomers knew what was waiting for them, they'd turn and run. He says that bread would give an orangutan indigestion. He says if Rowena's mother ever gives us another loaf of her freshly baked bread, he's going to drop it on her foot. He says he'll be very interested to see what happens to Rowena's mother's foot when her bread falls on it.

Anyway, this family has a crowd of kids. They range from little to fairly big, Rowena's mother says. She says she caught a glimpse inside the moving van and counted at least four beds. Maybe more.

"Where do they hail from?" Mrs. Sykes asked Rowena's mother. Mrs. Sykes has a little beard, sort of like a goat, and is hard-of-hearing. She lives alone and takes a bath in the spring and in the fall. When she was a girl, her grandmother told her that too much water dries out the complexion. People tend to avoid Mrs. Sykes. She shouts so people will be sure to hear her.

"I said, 'Where do they hail from?' " Mrs. Sykes asked again, at the top of her voice, when Rowena's mother didn't answer her right off.

"They're outa staters!" Rowena's mother shouted

back. In Maine anyone who isn't born and bred in Maine is an outa stater.

"'That so?" Mrs. Sykes shook her head despairingly. "Well, might's well try to pretend they're good as you and me. Might's well close our eyes to the fact they're different and just smile and say, 'Howdy.' God moves in mysterious ways. Maybe He's testing us, wants to see how charitable we can be. Wants to sit back and watch us love our fellowman." Mrs. Sykes pulled at her little beard the way she does when she's puzzled.

"Can't say as I see why He wants to push us like that, though. I put a dollar in the plate last Sunday. Didn't expect any thanks. Didn't expect a load of foreigners in my front yard, neither!" she said. Then she waddled over to her 1949 Chevvy that has its original tires, and drove home. Everybody in town knows Mrs. Sykes. They try to stay out of her way as much as possible. She drives smack in the middle of the road, to avoid accidents, sounding her horn all the way. Her horn makes a funny little bleating noise that also sounds like a goat. Mrs. Sykes raises goats, which may account for her resembling one. They say people begin to look like their dogs after a while. So that would explain Mrs. Sykes and her beard. Anyway, she was born and raised in Maine.

"Never been outa state but the once," she brags. "Didn't want to go then, but it was our honeymoon and my husband had relatives over in New Hampshire owed him money. So we went. Didn't stay but the one night, though. Left right after they paid up. He charged 'em interest too. Oh, you shoulda heard 'em when he charged 'em interest." Then she'd shake her head, and her little beard would tremble with admiration at her husband's cunning.

Rowena couldn't wait to fill Betty and me in on the details of the newcomers.

"There's a girl about our age," Rowena said. "Got this real cute figure, from what I could see, and she's got curly hair. Permed, most likely." Rowena rolled her eyes around in her head so vigorously I was fearful they might fly out of their sockets and land in the road.

"Maybe this new girl would be good for our club," I suggested. "Lord knows we got room."

Betty said, "She's from outa state," as if that disqualified the new girl from joining.

"So what?" I said. "I think we should go over there and say hi. How would you feel if you were new in town and nobody even came over and said hi? Wouldn't you feel rotten?"

"I guess," Rowena said doubtfully. We don't get too many strangers moving in around here, and most folks get clutched at the very idea.

"Well," I said, "I don't know about you two, but I'm going." So we went. The moving van was just pulling out as we arrived. It was a move-yourself type. A big, burly red-faced man was driving. He waved to us and we waved back. Rowena's mother was just pulling in, her loaf of freshly baked bread tucked under her arm, her black shoes with the heels carrying her swiftly down the driveway, past the shed where the previous tenants kept their chickens, past the little heaps of car parts scattered here and there, as if for decoration, and onto the front porch, right up to the door.

The yard was deserted. There was an old blue truck out in back and piles of empty boxes and cartons sitting on the porch. Just as Rowena's mother lifted her fist to bang on the door, a dog came around the side of the house, walking slowly on stiff legs, growling a little deep in his throat to show who was boss.

"Oh, oh," Betty said. We watched. The dog stood still. So did Rowena's mother. A boy who looked like he had adenoids came to the door.

"My ma's not home," he said, pushing his face against the screening, which billowed out like a sail filled with wind. "She said not to let nobody in." He stared out at Rowena's mother and us. The dog sighed and flopped down and fell immediately asleep.

"I'm your new neighbor," Rowena's mother said in her sweet company voice. She held out the bread. "Welcome," she said. "I baked this fresh this morning. For you all. Welcome."

He stared at her some more. His dark little eyes were

full of hostility. "We can't take stuff from strangers," he said at last. "My ma said you never know what might be inside. Razor blades. Pizen." That's what he said: "Pizen." We figured he meant poison. We could see Rowen's mother's back stiffen. She has been known to fly off the handle.

"Besides," the boy said, "we're vegetarians," almost like other folks say, "We're Presbyterians."

For once, Rowena's mother was speechless. "Let's go," Betty whispered. That seemed like a good idea. We turned on our heels.

"Where's the dump?" a loud voice demanded.

"What?" I said, looking around. A girl about our age, with plenty of bouncy curls, stood on the steps. "Where's the dump?" she repeated crossly. "Where's it at? First thing we always do, we find where the dump's at. You'd be surprised what you find laying around a dump. Why, once we fixed ourselves up with a bed and a davenport and a chiffonier. All three. Plus"—she dragged out her voice to get our attention—"plus a whole roll of Christmas wrapping paper. Silver and clean as a whisker." She smiled. "Was that at Bradford Falls, where we found that?" she asked the boy with adenoids. He said something we couldn't catch.

"Anyways," the girl said impatiently, "where's it at?"

I made my voice as loud as hers as I said, "Turn left at the top of the hill, go along till you come to Cross

Road, take another left, follow that to the end. You can't miss it."

"O.K." She nodded and didn't say, "Thanks."

"My name's Schuyler Sweet," I said. I would've shaken hands, but she had the look about her of turning people down so I didn't. Her dress was real short, and her legs were bare and purplish from the cold. She was eleven, twelve, thereabouts and she already had a figure. None of the rest of us did, although Rowena liked to think *she* did.

"What kind of a name's that? I never heard of a person named that before," she said.

"Best kind." I put her in her place. "What's yours?"

"Nell Foster," she said with a practiced toss of her curls. "These here . . ." Her arm swept behind her, taking in the crowd of kids who had gathered behind her. There were only three of them, it turned out, but they seemed like a crowd.

"They're my kin."

Behind me I could hear Betty and Rowena breathing heavily. Take them out of their own backyard and they're all thumbs, if you get my meaning.

"That's a lot of kin," I said. Nell Foster didn't answer. She stepped smartly back inside the house and shut the door in my face. Rowena's mother snatched up her loaf of bread and marched back down the driveway, head high, shaking with rage.

After a minute we followed. At the end of the property I stole a backward look. The place looked deserted. Even the dog was gone. It was almost as if I'd imagined the lot of them.

"Come on," Betty called. "We better get out of here. They're outa staters. What can you expect?" I followed them down the narrow dirt road, but I kept my distance so that if anyone happened to look out of the window of the house they wouldn't think we were together.

5

"*Mama, I don't want you to go,*" *Sidney said. The boys* and I were watching my mother pack her suitcase. She's leaving tomorrow. My father is driving her to Portland to get a plane to Boston, where she'll catch her flight to Africa.

"I'll only be gone two weeks, Sidney. I'll be back before you know I'm gone." She swept him up in a big hug. "And I'll bring you back something special. What would you like?" She put Sidney down and held up a flowered skirt. "I hate this skirt," she said. "Never should have bought it. What would you like, Sidney?"

Sidney concentrated on what he'd like her to bring him. "How about a little alligator?" he said at last. "One I could fit in my pocket. Then I could take him to kindergarten for show-and-tell. I bet it would be the only alligator in school that ever came from Africa. I would like that." His big eyes never left her face. I knew Sidney would have a bad time the first couple of days my mother was gone. He always did. I never told her how much Sidney missed her because I knew it would make her feel bad. This was the first trip she'd taken since she and Dad had gotten divorced.

My father said from the doorway, "Don't forget to tell your mother to leave us her itinerary. I want to know how to reach her at all times. Just in case."

"Dad," I said. "There she is. You tell her." My father had been shut up in his studio all morning working on Plotsie. I could tell by his hair. It stood up in peaks, like well-whipped cream. Before they got divorced, my mother and father told us that didn't mean they didn't still care about each other. They did, they said. My mother told me when she got back from her trip she might move into a small house and take us kids with her. "What about Dad?" I said.

"He'll manage," she said, avoiding my eye. "He'll get

along fine. Your father doesn't really need people. You'll see."

I didn't believe her then, and I don't believe her now.

"I'm hoping Angus will come back with me," my mother said directly to my father. Angus is the great white hunter she told me she was in love with. He's from Australia, only she met him the last time she went to Africa. "I want him to meet the children and see Maine. I want you to meet him too," she said. "I want to know what you think of him."

"Don't be too determinedly modern about this, Mary," my father said, patting his pockets for a pack of cigarettes, forgetting for the moment he'd given them up. "I'm not sure I want to meet Angus."

My mother got red in the face. "I want the children to meet him and tell me what they think of him. Tad, you haven't said what you want me to bring you." She cupped Tad's chin in her hand. "What is your heart's desire, darling?" she asked him.

Tad is not very talkative. Some days you can count the number of words he says on the fingers of both hands. My mother and father worried about him when he was little. He didn't start to talk until he was almost four. That's very late to start talking. When he finally broke down, he said, "No, thank you. I don't want any." Then he shut up for another week or ten days until he had something else worth saying.

Now he said, "I want an elephant tusk, Mama. Not a big one. A medium-size one. Please." Then he clamped his lips tight shut, a sign he was signing off until further notice.

My mother made out a list: Sidney, one small alligator. Tad, one medium-size elephant tusk.

"How about you, Sky?" she asked me. I felt like saying, "Leave Angus where he's at," but I knew that would hurt her feelings. So I said, "Oh, I don't know, Mom. How about a warthog? They're kind of cute." I liked the idea of having my own warthog.

"If I had a warthog, we could make him the mascot of our club," I said.

"What club's that?" my mother said, checking the camera she was planning to take with her.

"This club we've started. It's called the Chum Club. It's me and Rowena and Betty and maybe the new girl. We didn't ask her yet."

"I heard there was a new family down the road." My mother rolled up a pair of chinos and tucked them in a corner of her suitcase. She's an expert packer. A good thing. She does a lot of packing. "That's nice there are some new children around. What time should we leave in the morning?" she asked my father, who lounged in the doorway, propped against the doorframe, regarding her quizzically.

"About nine. I want to get home to get some work

done. Sidney can stay with Mrs. Edwards. I'll pick him up there." Mrs. Edwards lives not far from us. Her children have grown. She loves having Sidney stay with her. She says it's like having her own grandchild. Her children are reluctant to commit themselves to parenthood, she told my mother.

"There's a lot of hogwash going on these days," Mrs. Edwards said when she told my mother she doubted she'd ever be a grandmother. "If you ask me," she said, "there's more hogwash going on than previously. If you ask me, there's too much talk and too little action going around these days." Mrs. Edwards was fond of saying, "If you ask me," although nobody ever got a chance to ask her anything because she was inclined to answer questions before they were asked.

That night we all ate together. My father was unusually quiet. My mother chatted and smiled and kept patting us. Except my father, of course. We had roast chicken and mashed potatoes and green beans. And apple pie for dessert.

"I'm going to miss you all," my mother said. Sidney got down from his chair and went off to his room. My mother and father exchanged looks, like in the days before they got their divorce.

"I could kick myself," my mother said. "How could I be so stupid?"

We heard Sidney keening away in his bed. "What's

his problem?" Tad demanded in an angry voice. "She's only going to be gone two weeks." Then he left the table too, and when I found him, he was lying in the empty, dry bathtub playing with his plastic dinosaurs.

I put my hand on the hot water faucet, pretending I was going to turn it on, trying to make him smile.

"I don't care if she's going," he whispered, closing his eyes. "She'll be back. Won't she? She said she'd be back. She always comes back." Here I was, halfway to twelve, and I felt like crying too. But I wasn't going to be a baby about my mother's going. I had to set an example for the boys.

Besides, it wasn't as if my father didn't take good care of us. He always does. I'm glad he works at home. Also, he's quite a good cook. His specialty is fried potatoes. Once in a while we pig out on his fried potatoes. He cooks us a meal and that's all we eat: fried potatoes. We can have all we can hold, he says. We eat until we're full, then he opens a jar of apple sauce or canned peaches for dessert. Once, in the summer, when my mother was away, he took us down to the dock to the Lobster Shack for a lobster dinner. It was so beautiful that night. The moon was full, and there weren't any bugs, and we sat on the deck and tied lobster bibs around our necks so we wouldn't get melted butter on ourselves. Eating lobsters is very messy. People came from miles around to eat at the Lobster Shack. When my father finishes eating a lobster, all that's left is a pile of shells. Being a Maine native, he knows how. It takes years of practice to really eat a lobster, he says.

It looks funny to see grown men and women eating with bibs on. I remember hearing the water lapping against the pilings. It was a night to remember, all right. All that was missing that time was my mother too.

6

A *swarm of kids was already at the bus stop when me* and the boys walked up there in the morning. There were the regulars: Ollie and Jerry Brown and the two Kimball girls. We said hi. In the distance I saw Nell Foster, trailed by three people. It wasn't until they got close that I saw they were all boys. They all looked like her. They wore clothes that were either too big or too small. Nell's curls were round and fat and perfect.

"Hello." I broke the ice. "Your hair looks nice."

She stood still, turning her head this way and that to show off the curls to best advantage.

"It's naturally curly," she said in a piercing voice.

"It is not!" the largest boy said in a half shout. She reached over and took a swipe at him. He ducked. The other two stood silent, picking at their noses with little cold fingers, snuffling, looking out across the field like they didn't care what went on.

"My mama has naturally curly hair too," Nell said, keeping her eye on the big boy. He opened his mouth. She lifted her closed fist. He closed it.

"I get my naturally curly hair from my mama," Nell went on. "My mama's a beautician," she added, as if the two were connected.

"That's nice," I said.

"When the hell's this bus get here anyway?" Nell said. The other kids kept quiet. They watched and listened, as if they were at a play and we were the actors.

I looked down the hill. "Any minute now. So why'd you move here? Your daddy in business here?" I made my voice sprightly and interested, the way you're supposed to with a new acquaintance.

"Oh, my daddy's gone," Nell said, gazing soulfully up at the sky. I took that to mean her daddy was in heaven. I felt bad I'd asked about him.

"I'm sorry," I said. "When'd he die?"

"He didn't *die*," she said impatiently. "He's gone. Flew

the coop. Took a powder. Maybe he'll be back." She shrugged. "Usually he comes back. If he can locate us, that is."

The bus chugged up the hill. Bill, the driver, swung the door open. "Cold enough for you?" he said. We all got in. "You new around here?" he asked Nell.

"We live yonder," she said, herding the three boys in front of her like they were sheep. "They told us to go on down to the school today. A lady came to our house and told us that." Nell flicked her eyes, checking out the other kids in the bus. "Otherwise, we wouldn'ta gone. I got better things to do," she announced.

"Sit down and keep quiet and we'll all be pals," Bill said, closing the door with a whoosh, starting up.

Nell directed the two little boys to a seat, then she sat directly behind them. The big boy went to the back and sat on his spine, frowning out the window. I sat next to Nell, although she didn't ask me to.

"What grade you in?" I asked her.

"I'm not sure." Slowly, with great attention, she took off her mittens. She was the only one who wore mittens. Her brothers' hands were bare. I couldn't help noticing her fingernails were painted green.

"Maybe fifth, maybe sixth," she went on, holding her hands up, inspecting her fingernails with care. "I'm very smart, you know." She fixed me with her speckled yellow eyes, eyes that put me in mind of a cat's eyes.

"My uncle lives with us," she informed me. "My Uncle Joe. He helps us out sometimes. He drives a truck, you see. An egg truck," she added in a lofty tone, trying to impress me. I was more impressed by her green fingernails.

"You know he's got to be a good truck driver if they let him drive one of those huge egg trucks loaded down with eggs." She gripped my arm with fingers like steel. She was very strong. "Now don't you know that?" she demanded.

From his seat across the aisle, Tad said, "Daddy said you better wait for me after school, Sky. He said you better not go to somebody's house, that you should wait for me." Tad talks a lot when he's nervous.

"I know," I said. "I won't go without you." Tad settled back in his seat. As long as nothing happens to change the plans, he's all right.

"That's my brother," I told Nell.

"I got three brothers," she said. I noticed she didn't ask *me* any questions. "There's the two littles, then the big guy. Him and me are only a year apart. I only hit them when they get out of line. They know not to mess with me. I keep them in line, all right."

"I like your fingernails," I said. "How'd you get 'em that color?"

She leaned toward me. I could smell her hair. It smelled of hair spray.

"That's nothing," she bragged. "You oughta see my toenails." There didn't seem to be much to say to that so I didn't say it. When the bus pulled up in the school parking lot, I asked Nell if she wanted me to show her where the principal's office was. She shrugged. "I'll find it," she said. "Come on, you," and she herded her brothers in front of her. If it'd been me, I would've been shaking in my shoes. A new school on the first day is a nervous-making thing. Ask anybody. But not Nell. I stared at her as she marched her brothers in the door, her ringlets bouncing, mittens stuffed in her pocket so everyone could see her green fingernails.

7

In the lunchroom Nell was surrounded by boys; thin, fat, short, tall, you name it. Older boys, like Tommy Minch and Roger Brough. Roger already had a mustache. I heard he trimmed it in the boys' room with his mother's manicure scissors. He and Tommy had been left back so many times nobody could remember what grade they were in. Boys whose names I didn't even know, and I'd been in the same school all my life. Well, since kindergarten, anyway.

"What's she doing, giving away dollar bills?" Rowena

huffed, her nostrils flaring as she watched Nell through slitted eyes. Her jaws moved as if they were keeping time to music as she chewed her bologna sandwich. "I'm surprised they stand for that sort of thing in the lunchroom."

Betty pressed her lips together and said, "I never." The words came out as if they'd been squashed along the way. "I absolutely never." She didn't say what she never. She opened her lunch bag and peered down into it, holding her head back on her long neck as if she expected something live to spring out at her.

"She just got here," Rowena said in an aggrieved tone, "and would you please look at her. She must think she's a TV personality. Who does she think she is!" Rowena tossed her head, and the odor of vinegar filled the air.

"My mother says they're only renting," Rowena said. A burst of laughter ricocheted around the room. I saw one of the boys, who only last week had stuffed a note down Rowena's sweater, making goo-goo eyes at Nell. Rowena saw him too, and although at the time she'd told me she thought he was terribly immature, I noticed her watching him watching Nell, and her face was not friendly. I ate my cream cheese and nut sandwich and thought about the fickle hearts of men. About which I know zilch.

"So what if they're only renting?" I said. "I think she'd be very good to have in the club."

"In what way?" Betty asked, sounding like a dowager at a tea party. "In what way could she possibly be good to have in the Chum Club?" She always calls it by its full name, Chum Club. Just because it was her idea. She thinks it sounds classier that way.

"For one thing, she knows how to find stuff at the dump. You heard her. And we need stuff to sell. That's what a yard sale's all about, dummy. Items to sell. You heard what she said about the davenport and the bed and the chiffonier."

I had them. I could tell by the light of pure, unadulterated greed shining from their eyes that I had them by the tail.

"I don't even know what a chiffonier *is*," Rowena said, but her voice lacked its customary ring of authority.

"It's big," I said. I didn't know what a chiffonier was either. I'd meant to look it up in the dictionary last night, and I'd forgotten. "We could get a bundle for big stuff like that."

"Renters"—Rowena got back on course—"are ships that pass in the night. They are transients. Furthermore"—she extracted a piece of bologna from between her teeth and tossed it over her shoulder as if she'd made a wish on it—"they are frequently deadbeats. They don't pay their bills. They have been known to skip town under cover of darkness, kiddo. Owing back rent. Plus other bills. My mother says renters are very irresponsible people."

"You're a troublemaker," I told her. "And full of hogwash." And so's your mother, I wanted to say and didn't.

"My mother says if those people ever came to her on bended knee, she'd turn the other cheek. She is a very forgiving person, my mother."

"Why would they come to your mother on bended knee?" I said. The very idea made me laugh.

"All right for you." They both got sore. Betty said, "She's a newcomer, and we've been friends for life."

"Someday you might be a newcomer," I said. "I hope people are nicer to you than you are to her."

"Since when are you known for charity?" Rowena snapped.

"She's different. She could teach us things. Besides," I said, "she's got IT."

"She's got what?" Rowena asked irritably.

"IT," I said. "That's what they called sex appeal in the olden days."

"How do you spell it?" Rowena asked.

"I-T," I told her. "How else? Also known as OOMPH. Spelled just the way it sounds," I said, in case she wanted to know how to spell that word too. "Isn't that a neat word? I love it."

Rowena and Betty said, "OOMPH," a couple of

times, to get the feel of it. They liked it too.

"I like OOMPH better than IT," they both decided.

Whatever it was called, whatever it was, Nell obviously had it. We obviously didn't. I suspected Rowena was going to have a tough time digging up somebody to stuff notes down the back of her sweater as long as Nell was around. I was glad about that. It didn't matter to Betty and me because we didn't expect it. But Rowena had gotten impossible, more so than usual, since the notes started coming. It would do her good to be taken down a peg or two.

"Forget about her." Betty's eyelids fluttered madly. "We don't want her in the club anyway. She can join one of the other clubs."

Our class is loaded with clubs. There's the Sci-Fi Club for people who are into science fiction. They run around talking gobbledygook, a strange-sounding language that is their idea of how people from outer space talk. No one but them can understand it.

Then there's the Y Club, whose members swim in the Y pool all year round. They go around all winter with icicles hanging from their ears, smelling of chlorine. The Fan Club has the most members, although some dropped out when the postal rates went up. They write fan letters to Farrah Fawcett and Cher—people like that. Sometimes they get form letters back, saying, "Thanks for your nice letter." One girl wrote a long letter to Joan Crawford, telling her she'd heard about all the mean things Joan's daughter wrote about her mother and that she didn't believe a one. She told Joan she admired her and thought she was the world's greatest actress. She said in her letter, "Please send me an autographed picture of you." Then for weeks she rushed home from school to see if Joan had written back. Finally someone clued her in to the fact that Joan was dead. And had been for some time. She cried for two whole days, she felt so bad. Then she wrote a letter to Joan's daughter telling her what she thought of her for writing such nasty things about her own mother, closing with "Please send me an autographed copy of your book." She mailed the letter to the publisher of the book. She never heard another word.

After school Tad was waiting for me at the bus stop. Nell passed us by, her brothers bringing up the rear in a little dark clump, like a swarm of bees, scowling at everything and everyone. I heard a boy I knew say to his friend, "She's some nice," and I knew he meant Nell.

The bus was ready to leave. Bill sounded the horn, and Nell came running. "Hey," I said, friendly like. She pretended she didn't hear me. All the way home I heard her giggling and talking, her voice fast and high. Tad and I got off at our stop. Nell and her brothers stayed in their seats.

"End of the line," Bill said.

"How about taking us to our front door?" Nell said in a flirtatious way he couldn't take amiss. Bill laughed and said, "Out," and Nell put out her tongue at him saucily. I watched her going toward her house, the brothers trailing, kicking at dirty clumps of snow left in the rutted road, kicking at them like the snow was a ball and they were playing a game.

Tad and I checked our mailbox. "It's too soon for a postcard," Tad said.

"She's not even there yet," I said.

"Hey!" I heard someone shout. I looked up. It was Nell.

"You want to see our house?" she yelled.

She wanted to be friends, after all. "Sure," I shouted back. I like to see people's houses. "Come on, Tad." I pulled him along with me. Nell ran on ahead and skinned inside before we reached the porch. Her brothers had disappeared.

The door opened and Nell poked her head out through the crack.

"It'll cost you a nickel," she said, holding out her hand.

"What?" I wasn't sure I'd heard her right.

"If you want to see inside, it'll cost you a nickel," she repeated, eyeing us. "'Course, if you only want to look in the window, it'll be a penny." She jerked her thumb at Tad. "He can look for free," she said grandly.

"I don't have any money," I said. I never heard of

anyone charging money to look at their house. Except for house tours in the summer, which are another way to get money out of the tourists. They hold tours of the old houses in town, and they charge five or ten dollars, something wicked like that, for people to tour the insides. These tours are very popular and raise lots of money for different charities. The ladies who tour the old houses can't wear high heels on account of the high heels poke holes in the old floors and old rugs. I never saw so many ladies in hats wearing sneakers in one place in my life as when those hordes of tourists traipse through the old houses.

Nell inched the door closed until nothing but a thin, pie-shaped piece of her face looked out at me. "Next time you have some money, come on back and I'll let you in. The two of you. Only a nickel for both." Her eyes gleamed.

"It's a bargain," she said. "Any way you look at it. Only a nickel for both," and the door closed and she was gone.

8

"I've invited Pamela for supper," my father said, browning onions and garlic in a skillet. "All right with you?"

"Sure," I said. Last year my father taught a night course in drawing at the high school. He said he'd never do it again because it took too much time out of his work schedule, but that, for a one-shot thing, it had been fun and interesting. Well, Pamela had been one of his students, and ever since, whenever my mother was away, Pamela oozed her way into our house. Usually at suppertime. If there's one person who gives me a royal pain, it's Pamela. She calls herself an artist, but I don't think she sells anything she paints. Which are pictures of the coastline. Water and rocks, rocks and water. That's it.

I'm positive Pamela wears false eyelashes. Once I had this overpowering urge to reach out and pull them, to see if they'd come off. But I didn't. The first time she came, I asked my father why he'd invited her.

"Oh, I didn't invite her," he said. "She just showed up. So I asked her to stay. I think she's lonely." Honestly. For an intelligent man, my father is a pushover. But he has a kind heart. I wish some of it would rub off on me.

"You want me to make some dessert?" I said.

"Pamela doesn't eat dessert."

"I mean for me and the boys. Some Jell-O, maybe? With whipped cream."

"Pamela doesn't use cream."

Well, bully for her. "How's Plotsie doing?" I asked, to get off the subject of Pamela.

"I'm sorry to say Plotsie seems to be at a standstill. I'm trying to think up a new sequence for him to get involved in."

"Dad," I said. We almost never get a chance to talk, what with the boys around. "Dad, do you think you and Mom will ever get together again?"

He threw some hamburger into the pot and stirred. "I don't know," he said. "Your mother's a free spirit. There's no sense trying to hold her when she wants to be off. No sense at all."

"But we're her children," I said. "She's got no business going off and leaving us." I tried to keep the anger I felt out of my voice and wasn't too successful.

He looked at me, surprised. "Why don't you tell her that?" he said. "Maybe she'd listen to you."

Sidney came in. "Mrs. Edwards gave me a teddy bear," he said. "She says it's mine. It's got holes where its eyes was."

"Were," my father said.

"Were what?" Sidney asked, puzzled.

"Eyes were. Not eyes was."

Tad wandered through on his way to the bathroom. I could tell because he was clutching himself. Tad always clutches himself when he has to go to the bathroom. My mother says he'll outgrow it. I certainly hope so. For his sake.

A car pulled up outside. Pamela breezed in without knocking. She must feel pretty secure with my mother out of the country. She pressed cheeks with my father, who was busy making salad dressing. "Watch it," he cautioned. "You almost made me spill the vinegar."

She drew back and said, "Sorry." Then she said, "Hi, kids." Tad stepped up his pace and kept on walking and clutching. Sidney said he had to go check on his teddy bear.

"What can I do to help?" Pamela said in that way people have when they expect to be told, "Absolutely nothing."

"How about cleaning the oven?" I said. "It's a mess." I laughed in a phony way to show her I was only kidding. It's true that I hate phoniness, as I said, but am sometimes guilty of it myself.

Pamela shot me a look loaded with daggers behind my father's back.

"I can always set the table," she said. "If you show me where you keep the knives and forks." She's only been here for supper about ten times.

I heard someone knocking on the back door and went to see who it was.

"My mama says can we borrow a cup of sugar and some eggs," Nell said, stepping into our mud room as if she belonged. "We're baking us a cake."

"Dad," I said, "this is our new neighbor, Nell Foster. She moved into the Johnsons' house."

My father wiped his hands on his pants and shook Nell's hand. "How are you?" he said. I explained what she wanted, and he said, "Help yourself." She followed me into the pantry and took him at his word.

"I'll just take some of these"—her hand dipped into the egg box—"and you might as well give me two cups of sugar. I like a real sweet cake. Oooooh, you got sprinklies," she said. "I just love sprinklies." She meant those colored things you sprinkle on top of cakes and cookies. She took a few handfuls of them and watched me as I put the eggs and the sugar into a bag. "I'll just load these into my pocket," she said, letting the sprinklies slide through her fingers and into her big pockets.

"Find what you want?" my father asked. Nell smiled and nodded, checking out our kitchen. Pamela stayed where she was, sitting at the kitchen table, drinking sherry, unable to find the knives and forks. I had the feeling Nell knew what brand of stove we had and what kind of soap powder we used.

"I hear my mama calling me," she said, and the door banged behind her. No thanks, no nothing.

"There's a kid who'll go places," my father said. "She has all the confidence of a great beauty."

Pamela fluttered her eyelashes. "Hard as nails," was her verdict. I watched Nell cross the snowy field between our houses and wished I had some of her nerve.

Next morning she was at the bus stop before us, her brothers looming darkly behind her, cracking their knuckles, chucking snow at the hawks skimming over the pine trees.

I figured she could say, "Hi," first. All she said was, "You sure don't look like your ma, do you? She's pretty."

"That's not my mother," I snapped. "My mother's in

Africa, taking photographs of wild animals."

Nell rolled her tongue around in her mouth, digesting what I'd said. Then she leaned toward me and said in a low voice, like she was a CIA agent telling me classified information, "My Uncle Joe's driving his truck all the way to Pennsylvania today. He might not be back for a week."

Africa was nothing compared to that, all right.

"Maybe he'll send you a postcard," I said in a super-nasty voice.

"If that wasn't your mama, who was it?" Nell said.

"A friend," I said, shrugging.

"Oh, yeah? Whose friend? Yours or your daddy's?" I was lucky. She didn't wait for an answer. Putting her hand over her mouth, she hissed at me, "I know how to kiss so's their tongue tingles."

"How?" I asked, wanting to hear her answer very much.

The bus rumbled to a stop just then, and Bill swung open the door.

"Cold enough for you?" he said, grinning.

Nell was up the steps and into the bus like a shot. She sat directly behind the driver's seat. I followed her in and walked to the back of the bus. If she wanted to tell me how she made their tongues tingle, she knew where to find me.

9

"*That lady I met at your house, she your daddy's girl friend?*" Nell asked me next day on the bus. She nudged me in the ribs and shot me a sly glance.

I pulled away from her a little. "My mother and father are divorced," I said. "But they live in the same house. We've got lots of room."

"I bet." She laughed. "Whatdya take me for, an idjit?"

I shrugged. "It's the truth. Take it or leave it. My father works at home. So does my mother, when she's not off on an assignment. They figure it's easier if we all stay under one roof." Why was I telling her all this? It was none of her business.

"Now I've heard everything." Up close I could see Nell's eyes were shadowed with smudged lavender circles, the color of a bruise. She smiled a little, and I saw one of her front teeth was chipped. She wore a dark skirt that came well below her knees, and a rusty old coat with only one button, which she kept clutching around herself. Her clothes weren't like other people's, but it didn't seem to bother her. She wore them with an air, as if they were designer jeans. I admired her for that. Most kids, including me, want to dress like everyone else. My mother says she hopes when I'm older I'll branch out, be different, be an individual. I'm not sure I can handle that.

Nell hitched herself closer as the bus swayed and groaned on its way homeward. "We might go out West this summer," she said in a confiding tone, letting me in on a secret. "One of my uncles has a place out there. He has about fifty horses. He said we could ride 'em any time we want. We're going to get us some of those slanty-heel boots, and I'm going to have a red silk neckerchief, and he promised us all some real cowboy hats."

"Where's his spread?" I said. I've seen plenty of cowboy movies on TV, and that's what they call it: a spread. For a second, Nell rolled her tongue around inside her mouth in a way she had that I would learn meant she was stalling for time, searching for an answer, not necessarily a truthful one.

"I'm not exactly sure," she said impatiently. "Out West, like I said."

"Out West is pretty big," I said. "How come I never see your mother around your place?" I'd been wanting to ask her that for some time.

"How come I never see yours?" she shot back.

"I told you. She's in Africa. She'll be back next week."

"Then I guess your daddy's girl friend will make herself scarce, huh?" she said.

"You don't care what you say, do you?"

"I don't blame your ma for taking off." She changed subjects. "I imagine she couldn't take it around here for long. If I lived in a poky old place like this here, I'd go nuts." She crossed her legs and rearranged her coat. "If I lived in any place forever and ever, I'd go beserk. Nothing ever happens here, does it?"

I scoured my brains to think of something that had happened, something exciting, within recent memory, and could think of nothing.

"It's so boring, living in one place your whole life." She stared at me. I could've sworn her eyes were light in color. But now they looked like dead coals set in her pale face.

"I like it." I defended my home town. "It's pretty. It's

the prettiest town in the state, you know." The minute I said the words, I was sorry.

"It is?" Nell's voice was high and harsh. "Who said?"

And, because I'd often wondered that myself, I got mad.

"It just is," I insisted. "Ask anybody."

"It's nothing but a little old hick town. Why, I bet they pull in the sidewalks when the sun goes down. Nothing to do all day long but count the campers going by," Nell said in a singsong. "Nothing to hear 'cept the dogs barking. It's the most boring place I ever been. And I been around, believe you me. I been in just about every state in the whole country."

"Hawaii?" I said, struck by a fit of genius. "Alaska?"

"Well, not them." She raised her shoulders in a shrug that showed Hawaii and Alaska didn't amount to a hill of beans. "They're Johnny-come-latelies, anyhow. They only been states a little while. But I been everywhere 'cept some of the M's."

"What're the M's?"

"You know. Mississippi, Minnesota, Michigan. Like that. Whenever we move, we get out the map and study where we're headed, where we're going. There's an awful lot of M's. Maryland, Missouri."

"And Maine, where you are right this minute."

"Right. I forgot Maine. I can't wait to get out of here. It's the ends of the earth, if you ask me."

Plenty of times I've wanted to go places, see things. But at that moment I loved Maine. My heart was suffocated with love for Maine.

"I'm sorry for somebody who keeps moving, always moving, never settling down," I said, striking back. I knew it was mean, but what she said about Maine, my home state, was mean too. "Folks who keep moving from place to place never make any friends. How do you make friends if you never light somewhere?"

"Friends!" Nell spat out the word. And then she laughed in a cruel way to let me know what she thought of friends. "That's the dumbest thing I ever heard." She jabbed a fingernail at me. "If you're smart," she said, "you get along without friends. You learn, kid, to get along on your own. I don't need anybody but me. I got me and the boys and that's it. That way I know who's on my side. With friends, you're liable to get it in the neck. That's how I see it. You can't trust friends. Anyone who counts on friends has to be cuckoo."

A shiver slid over me like somebody had walked on my grave. I never heard such talk. What if she was right?

"And I'll tell you something else, Miss Smarty." Nell's voice dipped low and angry in my ear. "I don't wear any pants if I don't want. If I don't feel like it. What do you think about that? Nobody tells me what to do. Nobody."

"Big deal," I said scornfully. "If I don't want to wear

pants, I don't either. I wear a skirt any time I feel like it."

Nell's raucous laughter made some kids turn and stare at us. "I don't mean pants pants," she hissed. "I mean underpants."

"I don't believe you," I said when I got hold of my voice.

Slowly, very slowly, in slow motion, she raised her long skirt so I could see she was telling the truth.

I swallowed and said, "Don't you get cold?" as matter-of-factly as possible.

She smoothed her skirt back down, and pulled her rusty old coat around her as if it had been made of ermine, and smiled at me in a way that let me know she had won whatever fight it was we'd had.

10

It was Saturday morning, nine a.m. We were in Row-
ena's basement. Rowena's mother stands guard over her
house like it was the Tower of London and the crown
jewels were hidden under the mattress. Nobody's allowed to sit on the beds, much less the couch. Every
piece of furniture is covered in a sea of plastic. There
are plastic runners on the rugs too, in case some outa
stater with car trouble knocks on the door asking to use
the telephone due to car trouble. Maine kids are trained
to leave their shoes outside practically before they're

toilet-trained, so as not to track in mud and snow. But Rowena's mother believes in being prepared. For anything.

Rowena's father is a traveling salesman and hardly ever home. Which makes it nice for Rowena's mother. That way she has one less person around to louse up her house.

So every time we go to Rowena's, we wind up in the basement, which smells of mildew and cat. Nell Foster sat, wearing her coat, in the big old hairy chair Rowena's cat always had her kittens in. She'd decided to join the Chum Club after all. No one was exactly sure who'd asked her. I know it wasn't me. But there she sat, in the only comfortable chair in the place, saying she'd join. Under certain conditions. She wanted to be chairman of the yard sale and also treasurer.

"Out of the question! Out of the question!" Betty shouted, whirling around like a dervish in full flight. Rowena looked befuddled and pushed her hair off her forehead so she could think better.

Nell sat still, waiting for silence. After the protests died down, she began to speak, so softly we had to lean toward her to hear what she said.

"I knew a lady, went to this yard sale," Nell said in a slow and draggy way. "She bought this rickety old chair for fifty cents." Nell paused, saw she had us, and continued. "She took that little chair home, let it rest some, then sold it at a yard sale of her own next week for five dollars." When she reached the end of her story, her voice was a little whispery thing that barely had the strength to work its way up her throat and out into the room.

We all looked at each other.

"What's that got to do with the price of onions?" I said.

"I'm just telling you," Nell said, very patient. "I'm a pro when it comes to yard sales. My services are very valuable. We been holding yard sales since I was no bigger'n a minute. My mama invented yard sales, as a matter of fact."

"She never," I said. "Nobody invented yard sales. That's stupid. People invent radium or electricity or the wheel, but they sure as shooting don't invent yard sales."

Nell said, "You got some big mouth, you know that?"

Betty and Rowena sat like two bumps on a log, lacing their fingers in and out, acting like they were being hypnotized. Which, in a way, they were.

"I'm going to tell you another story," Nell said in the same draggy voice, like she was a fortune teller reading your future in a crystal ball. "There was this lady who went to a yard sale, saw this terrible old chippy china dish. She took a fancy to that dish and said she'd give ten cents for it. Not a penny more. So the man owned the dish said, 'Oh, shoot, all right, you can have that for ten cents. Go away and don't bother me no more,' the man said. And didn't that lady turn right around and sell that chippy old dish to some museum for around a thousand dollars."

Betty and Rowena gasped, sounding like the air being let out of some old tires. I didn't make a sound.

Nell frowned at me. "Tell me how your mother invented yard sales," I said. "I'd like to hear."

"One day she was sitting there, not doing much," Nell said, shooting daggers at me, "and she said, 'Why don't we take a bunch of our old junk out of the attic and just throw it out in the yard and try to sell it. Simple as pie.' And that's how yard sales started."

"You're full of hot air," I told her.

That didn't seem to bother Nell. "Believe me or not," she said. "That's the way it was. What do I care if you believe me or not? What's it to me?"

"All right, come to order." Betty leaped to her feet, taking the reins in her hands one more time. "Now we get down to the nitty-gritty. We figure out what each one brings. I'm keeping a list of what everyone brings."

"What're you bringing?" Nell asked Rowena.

"Why," she said, "my mother's fur coat."

"What besides that?" I said.

"Listen," Rowena yelled at me, "that's a big item. How

many times do you see a fur coat at a yard sale?"

Betty and I exchanged looks. A fur coat is a fur coat, and there's no way around that.

"Everyone will bring one card table." Betty was writing fast now. "To display the goods on."

"What about guards?" Nell asked.

"Guards?"

"To keep stuff from being ripped off. Yard sales are great for pickpockets to operate in." Nell sounded like she knew. "Folks slip things into their pockets and take off. Either that or they say, 'I paid for it back there,' and make off with anything they want. You need big guys for guards. Guys who look like they'd tackle you if you steal anything. You got to strike fear into their hearts if they rip you off." She studied her fingernails. I'd told Betty and Rowena they were painted green. Today they were bare and pale.

"Whose yard we having this sale in?" I said.

"We haven't figured that out yet," Betty said. "My father says we can't have it in ours. He doesn't want the responsibility. Somebody might fall down in our yard, he says, then they'd sue us. If they broke a leg they might sue us for a lot of money, so he says we can't have it in our yard."

"Isn't that something!" Rowena cried. "My father says we can't have it either. We planted a new lawn last spring, and my father says if a mess of people tramped all over it, that new lawn would go down the drain so fast you wouldn't be able to see it disappear."

"I'll ask my father if we can have it in ours," I said. "He probably wouldn't mind."

"We best have it in mine," Nell said firmly. "That way we got my brothers to help us, and it doesn't make any difference what happens to our yard on account of it isn't ours."

The logic of her statement was unassailable. "How about Old Man Johnson, your landlord? Won't he care?" Betty thought to ask.

"What he don't know won't hurt him, that's for sure," Nell answered.

That was how we decided to hold the yard sale in her yard.

Then Nell took charge. "We can use our old pickup to travel to the dump in, pick up some stuff to sell," she said.

"Who'll take us?"

"If my Uncle Joe's not home, I'll drive," she said, fixing us with her steely glance.

"You drive? You're too young. They'd catch you for sure."

"I best steer clear of the main road, or they might," Nell said. "There must be a back way to get there."

Even I was overcome by the idea of Nell Foster driving the pickup to the dump. Rowena tiptoed halfway up the cellar stairs to make sure her mother wasn't listening at the top of the stairs, which she had been known to do.

"Wouldn't you be scared?" I said.

Nell lifted her shoulders and turned up her hands, as if to say, "Of what?"

"It's easy," she said. "I did it plenty of times. Me, I like to see the sights, keep moving. I don't want to be a stick-in-the-mud. Not me."

She stood up and pulled on her rusty old coat with the saggy bottom.

"I got to go," she said. "Yipe!" she cried, picking at herself. "I'm full of cat hairs. My mama'll have a fit. She's buggy on keeping a place clean. She will just have a plain old fit."

"Why, hello, Mother!" Rowena cried. Rowena's mother stood there, her face purple. From the expression on her face we knew she'd heard what Nell had said. Nell knew too. She licked her lips as if tasting something sweet.

"I'll just wash myself off real good when I get home," she said. "That way I'll be sure of no germs."

Rowena's mother whirled and thundered back upstairs, slamming the door behind herself. The cellar stairs, the walls trembled from the force of her blow.

"Refreshments are served!" Rowena's mother roared through the closed door. Nell said she couldn't stay. And all the time we were eating the freshly baked bread and drinking the cocoa, we heard pots and pans crashing around the kitchen. Rowena said her mother was out of sorts, probably due to what Nell had said about her housekeeping. She said not to pay her mother any mind, and we tried not to. It was sort of hard to hear ourselves talk with all that racket going on overhead, though.

11

Today we all got postcards from my mother. Even my father got one. Mine had a picture of a warthog on it. It said, "This reminds me of you. Ha-ha. See you very soon. Love and kisses, Mother." She always signs herself "Mother" when she sends us postcards. I like that: Mother. It's a nice word. We don't call her that, though. The boys call her Mama and I call her Mom. Daddy calls her Mary. He used to call her Hon. Sometimes he forgets and still calls her Hon. But not often.

"How will we know when she's coming home?" I asked him.

"She'll cable us," he said. "I'll drive to the airport to meet her."

"What if she brings *him*?" I didn't want to say Angus.

He looked at me, his eyes very bright and slick-looking. "Why, I'll bring him back with us. What did you think I was going to do, dump him off in the weeds by the highway?"

"No," I said. "I didn't think you'd do that."

"It's an idea, though," he said, and we both laughed.

I went around the house looking at everything with an eye to how much it might bring at our yard sale. When I asked my father if he had anything he didn't want that we could have, he rummaged through his drawers and came up with some shirts with frayed collars and a muffler with fringe at either end he said he'd never liked. It was a perfectly O.K. muffler and should bring a dollar easy.

The boys got into the spirit of the thing. Tad gave me a box of hardly used crayons, and a plush dog wearing faded overalls and a ratty old straw hat. "I hate him," Tad confided. "He smiles all the time." That seemed as good a reason as any for hating someone, and I didn't argue with him. Sidney chipped in his outgrown Donald Duck slippers, and, not to be outdone by Tad, he also threw in a set of plastic measuring cups and an old toothbrush.

I counted on my mother's going through a wild flurry of housecleaning when she got home. She has fits of clearing things out. Often she throws out a lot of stuff she wishes later she'd kept.

"Oh, dear, why didn't you stop me!" she wails when she goes looking for some treasure before she remembers she's given it away to some thrift shop. Or, sometimes, to me. I'm a pack rat. I never turn anything down. If she's given whatever it is she's looking for to me, I offer it back. She always says, "No, I'm not going to be an Indian giver. You keep it."

When Pamela came for supper last night, I asked her if she had anything she'd care to donate to our yard sale. She just looked down her nose at me. I always thought that was just an expression, but with Pamela it's true. She has the nose for it. She sort of sights down the barrel of her nose as if it were a rifle. And gives you this icy glance that's calculated to put you in your place and keep you there. It doesn't work with me, but I can see it would with some. Anyway, she looked down her nose and said, "Yard sales are *so* depressing. And so tacky, somehow." I said ours wasn't going to be either depressing or tacky. She looked at me and smiled a disbelieving smile. I could've smacked her. If she'd been my age I probably would've.

Nell said she could read bumps on people's heads and it might be good if we had a head-reading table at the sale. Betty and Rowena said that sounded more like a carnival than a yard sale and turned down the idea. I happened to mention it to the boys and they were thrilled. They began horsing around, feeling each other's heads.

"I got no bumps on mine," Sidney said. Later on in the evening, however, Tad belted Sidney with a small red fire engine. After the ruckus died down, I ran my hand over Sidney's head and told him he had a huge bump at last. Sidney was quite pleased and kept touching his bump, although it was tender, and saying, "I got a bump, after all." At that age, it takes very little to please them. That's one nice thing about being a little kid.

On Sunday I checked our attic. I found a box of linen napkins and tablecloths my mother had decided were too much trouble to iron, and a pile of old magazines. Then, to my delight, I discovered a ratty old chair pushed way back under the eaves. It was made of some scratchy fabric the color of dried blood. I sat in it for a while to get the feel of it. It didn't collapse and was, in fact, quite comfortable. I went downstairs to ask my father if he'd help me carry it down to the garage to put aside for the yard sale. He was on the living room floor drawing pictures for the boys.

"Dad," I said, "there's a terrible old beat-up chair in

the attic. Can I have it for our yard sale?"

"No," he said, not even taking time to think about it. "No."

"Why not?" I asked when I'd gotten over my surprise. I was sure he'd say it was all right.

"Well," he said, sitting back on his heels, "because that old chair holds many pleasant memories for me. It's the chair your mother and I were sitting in when I asked her to marry me."

That chair wasn't big enough for two people, I thought.

"Was Mom sitting on your lap?" I asked him.

"Yes," he said. "Yes, she was, and her head was resting right here," and he put his hand to his shoulder to show us where our mother's head had been. "She wore a pink dress, and she cried when I asked her. She said she wasn't sure she loved me. She thought she did, she said, but she wasn't sure. She wasn't sure what being in love felt like. She'd never been in love. Well, I had, once or twice, but never like this. I was afraid if she spent more time trying to make sure she loved me, she might change her mind entirely, so I said, "Of course you love me," and I was so sure, so positive I was right, she agreed to marry me the following week."

The boys and I were in some kind of trance. Sidney plugged up his mouth with his thumb and crawled into my father's lap, what there was of it. A real lap is possible only when a person sits in a chair or on a couch. My father was sitting on the floor, so his lap wasn't what it should be. Still, there was room for Sidney. A tiny smile worked its way around his thumb, and Sidney settled back as if he were getting ready to listen to a new story, a fairy tale he hadn't heard before.

Our father had never told us such a romantic story in his whole life. He couldn't have made it up. He was our father, and we didn't think of what or how he'd been before he was our father. Everybody is somebody else before they're a father, don't forget. The idea of my mother and father sharing the chair, the wonderful way they'd shared it, was quite overwhelming. If we all sat very still, maybe he'd forget we were there and his story would continue. It was as if he were talking to himself.

"I've often thought," he said slowly, "that I shouldn't have pressed her. I should have let her think it through. She was young. She wanted to see the world, taste things she'd never tasted. I'd been in the army and I'd seen the parts of the world I wanted to see. I was ready to settle down. I made her think she couldn't live without me. If she'd done what she wanted and then settled down, maybe she'd be happier now. Not so restless."

Sidney made his little slurping sounds. Tad and I stared into the fire. As he leaned against me, Tad sighed, a long, deep sigh.

"You have to let people do what they will," my father

said. "In letting them go, you bind them to you. That was my mistake. I thought that if I held her to me by marrying her, she'd be mine forever. It doesn't work that way."

My father was not a person who often let his children or anyone else see inside his heart. We were afraid to move, to break the spell. A log popped and scattered sparks on the hearth and over onto the rug. We scrambled up to kick the sparks back inside the fireplace. When we sat down again, it was too late.

"Well," my father said, "time to get back to work." He left us there, the boys and me. I felt very old. I wondered what he would have said if the log hadn't popped. What secrets would he have told us?

Tad said, "Read us a Curious George, Sky?" and I said I would.

"What happened at the end?" Sidney said. His eyelids were drooping. He was almost asleep.

"I haven't read the story yet, dopey," I told him.

"No," he said. "I mean what happened at the end of Daddy's story?"

"I don't know," I said.

12

My mother's been gone six days now. Almost a week.
Only eight more days until she comes home.

"Is Mama coming home with him?" Tad asked me.
He meant Angus.

"I don't know," I said. Which was true. Tad shot me
a wary glance out of his unblinking eyes. He thought I
was lying. I can always tell when Tad thinks I'm lying.
There's something about that wary look of his that
makes you think you might be lying even when you
know you're telling the truth.

Pamela's coming for supper again tonight. I think she invites herself. I don't think my father wants her to come that often. "How come she doesn't ask you to her house for supper?" I asked my father. "How come she doesn't ask us all to her house? She always comes here." I try not to let my father know how I feel about Pamela. I think I do a pretty good job of concealing my feelings. It's not easy.

"Pamela is probably the world's worst cook," my father said.

"Well, then," I said, "why doesn't she learn? She could go to cooking school." She's lazy. That's why she doesn't learn how to cook.

I read the boys a story every night before they go to bed. Their favorite is Curious George. They like the one about Curious George having a paper route. He folds the papers into the shape of a little boat. Then he sails the paper boats on a pond. The book has a little diagram showing how to fold papers into boats. Now Tad can hardly wait until he has a paper route. His customers will have to get used to having their papers delivered in boat form, I guess. Also, Sidney thinks it'd be neat if my mother brought him a monkey instead of a little alligator. I forgot to mention that Curious George is a monkey. Sidney thinks we should call up my mother in Africa so he can change his order.

"I could feed him bananas," Sidney said, talking

around his thumb. Try talking with your thumb in your mouth if you want to know what Sidney sounds like. Either a Russian or a Chinese. Take your pick.

"That's what monkeys eat, bananas," Sidney said. "I could take him to show-and-tell. I think a monkey'd be more fun than an alligator. What do you think?" He leaned on my knee and looked up at me, his little face so serious. Sidney cracks me up. He really does.

"Well," I said, "a monkey's more like a person than an alligator. If you want a pet that's like a person, I guess a monkey would be a good idea."

"He could wear my pants when I grow out of them," Sidney said. "And my pajamas. And my sneakers. And my underwear. And my . . ."

Once started, there was no stopping him. He darted back and forth to his bedroom, carrying armloads of his clothes, which he stacked in a towering pile.

My father looked on, bemused, as Sidney stuffed all his belongings into a shopping bag.

"Sidney, you're too young to go away for the weekend," my father said. "Put that stuff back until you get a little older. Put it back until your mother gets home. She can handle this. I've got Plotsie into a situation that neither he nor I seem to be able to get out of. And I've got supper to get. My mind is befuddled."

"Do you *like* being a father?" Sidney asked, after some thought.

My father said of course he did. "I just wondered," Sidney said.

"You want me to fix supper?" I asked.

"No," my father said. "I can handle it. But thanks anyway." My specialty is spaghetti with clam sauce. We've had it quite a lot since my mother went away. Last time I added some hot pepper flakes to jazz it up. Those little flakes don't look like much, but do they ever pack a wallop! Dad and the boys choked and coughed and carried on. I finished all mine. It brought tears to my eyes, but I wasn't going to admit defeat.

Tad tugged at my sleeve. "I've got something to show you," he said.

"Is it a secret or can you show it to me here?"

My father was checking the refrigerator, and Sidney was off in his room, humming loudly, opening and closing drawers. We were alone. Tad opened his mouth. "See. Another one." He waggled his front tooth with his tongue.

"Can I feel?" I said. He nodded.

"It's hardly loose at all. You won't be losing that one for a while," I reassured him. "Probably not until after Mama gets home."

"You think so?" Tad said anxiously. "If it comes out and I put it under my pillow, somebody might take it." Tad gave me a dark look. "This time if he lays a finger on it, he's gonna get it. Pow!" The flow of words stopped, but from the fierce glint in his eye, I knew he meant what he said. Sidney had better not flush this one down the toilet.

"We'll figure out something, Tad," I said, patting him. "Don't worry."

Sidney showed up, huffing and puffing, dragging an old ski jacket with a zipper that didn't work. "He can have this," he said. "For when it gets cold."

"This is going to be the best-dressed monkey in the whole State of Maine," I told him.

You'd think as long as Pamela comes to our house so often for supper she'd bring something. A deck of cards or a candy bar. Something. She has never once brought us anything. Some people grow on you. You don't like them at first but you get to like them when you know them better. Pamela is just the opposite. I liked her all right at first, but she's been going downhill steadily ever since. I decided to give her one last chance to win my heart. I opened the drawers we kept the knives and forks in and left them open. So she'd have no trouble finding them after she asked what she could do to help, and I said, "Set the table," and then she couldn't possibly come back with "Where do you keep the knives and forks?" because they'd be sitting there, staring out at her. With people like Pamela, you have to stay one step ahead all the time. Lazy people will do almost anything to get out of doing things. I hate lazies.

At last I heard a car outside. It was Pamela. Right on time, probably suffering from hunger pains. Sidney had just discovered an old coloring book. Each page bore a big slash of color across the pictures he was supposed to color. Just one big slash.

"Look at this," he commanded, showing it to me. "I must've did this when I was just a little baby." His voice was loaded with scorn. He tossed the coloring book into his shopping bag along with his discarded clothing intended for his monkey and staggered around the room, looking like a helper from the Salvation Army.

"Hi, ducks!" Pamela greeted us. "I brought you a pressy." What do you know.

The boys descended upon her, shouting, "What is it?" forgetting, for the moment, that she wasn't their favorite person. She had brought us a half gallon of ice cream. The cheap kind, I'm sorry to say, the kind that has more air and ice in it than cream. I know that's looking a gift horse in the mouth, but it's true. She must've leaned into the frozen food compartment and thought, Those little monsters will never know the difference. She was wrong. I knew.

"Thank you," I said.

"What kind is it?" Tad asked.

"Why, Tad," Pamela cooed, "can't you read that? A big boy like you. See, that's a C, then that's an H," and so on, giving Tad a spelling lesson that humiliated him and made him clamp his mouth shut as tight as any clam.

I kept waiting for Pamela to say, "What can I do to help?" in that special voice of hers. She didn't say it. She sat on one of the kitchen stools watching my father cook supper.

"How long till we eat, Dad?" I said.

"Not long. Ten, fifteen minutes."

I looked over at her. She was drinking sherry out of one of my mother's good glasses, swinging her foot, admiring her knees. I could tell setting the table was far from her thoughts.

What would my mother do? I wondered. Would she outwait Pamela, then, when the food was ready, spring into action, pretending she'd forgotten to set the table? Or would she simply say, "Here are the knives and forks. Go to it."

I decided my mother would take the direct approach. She usually does. "Here, Pam," I said, handing over the utensils. She'd told me to call her by her first name. I guess she thought that would make us friends. Also closer in age.

"Go to it," I said, smiling at her. "Pam."

Slowly, very slowly, she put down her glass and said "Why, of course, dear. I'd be glad to help. All you had to do was ask me." She uncrossed her legs, slid her bottom off the stool, and stood there, waiting, no doubt, for my father to say, "You do it, Sky. Pam's a guest," as he had on several occasions. This time he was silent. The boys watched as she laid out the knives and forks and spoons, lining them up as carefully as if she'd been a waitress at a classy restaurant.

I went into the bathroom, locked the door, and sat on the hard edge of the tub, smiling to myself. Then I turned on the cold water and washed my face hard, to bring myself into line. I laughed until I cried.

13

A *light, cold rain was falling Monday morning when* Nell and I met at the bus stop.

"Where's everybody?" I said. We were the only ones there. Tad had a cold and Sidney too. "Where's your brothers?" I asked Nell.

"Down with nothing," she said. "Watching TV all day long. She said they could stay home. She lets them get away with murder. Because they're boys." She shot a glance at me. "Mothers favor boys. I bet your mother does the same."

"No," I said truthfully. "She doesn't."

"Baloney. That's your story. If it was me, I'd have to be dying before she'd let me stay home from school. She's soft in the head when it comes to the boys. You can't tell me your mother's not the same."

I could tell by Nell's voice that this was one of her ornery days. Likely she'd contradict everything I said. She got like that.

I decided to change the subject. "Seems like spring will never come," I said brightly. "Blink your eyes and you miss it entirely."

"I'm hot." Nell flapped her coat in the stiff breeze blowing from the harbor. "I'm boiling." The gray sky hung down so low I was sure I could touch it, puncture it, bring down torrents on my head. The rain would turn to snow before long; the damp seeped into every opening it could find.

"I seen worse weather'n this plenty of times," she said. "Why, where we lived before, we had blizzards that could make you cry out with the cold. Temperature was down around thirty below, stayed there all winter. This is nothing."

"Winds get so strong around these parts," I countered, "they make your eyeballs jangle, they're so bitter." When it comes to one-upmanship with the weather, I'm a pro. Maine people like to talk about the weather. We figure as long as we're stuck with it, we might as well turn it into something to brag about—its awfulness, its severity. "I've seen storms," I told Nell, "where it hails and snows, thunders and lightnings all at the same time."

"All mothers are soft on boys." Nell ignored the weather and took up where she'd left off. "They just naturally take to sons more'n daughters." Her face was pinched and blue, and she stamped her feet in their raggedy sneakers to keep the blood going.

"My mother doesn't," I repeated.

"How would you know? She's never around for you to find out." When Nell was mean, her nose and chin got very pointed, almost like a witch's, and her eyes glittered in a special way.

"That's mean and it's not true," I said, trying to keep my voice under control. "I'd say you got out the wrong side of the bed this morning." I turned my back on her. I didn't have to listen to that guff.

"When I grow up"—Nell's voice changed, became soft and almost dreamy—"I'm not having any kids. You won't catch me being a mother. No siree."

She had a way of saying something outlandish one minute, something meant to shock or offend; then next minute she'd switch and say something to pull you back, almost like a fisherman with a fish on his line. Reel it out, let it struggle, try to work free, then deliberately reel it back in when it was almost gone. I turned halfway back to her, trying to see her face. She had pulled up her coat collar, and it shielded her face from me.

"Why not?" I had to ask.

"Who wants to be tied down?" she said in her old, fierce way. "You get yourself a mess of kids, you're saddled for life. Can't have any fun, always broke from buying shoes and medicine. Then they have the bellyache and keep you up all night, plus you have to take 'em to the doctor for shots and all, and that costs plenty. Kids are more trouble than they're worth, my ma says. She looks straight at me when she says it, too. There's lots of females in this world should never have kids." She fixed me with an icy stare.

"I suppose," I said, wanting her to continue, not sure of what she said.

"My ma never shoulda had us," she burst out. "She's sorry she did. 'Specially me. Said we were a mistake. All four of us. I told her if that was so, she shoulda learned from her first mistake and not gone on to make three more." We sat there and looked at each other, not talking.

"Then you know what she did?" Nell's eyes were enormous. I shook my head, not sure I wanted to know.

"She slapped me. In the face. Just plain up and slapped me." The lavender circles under Nell's eyes deepened in color.

"If she wasn't tied down with us kids, she said, she'd be famous," Nell went on.

"Doing what?" I asked, sorry at last for Nell. I couldn't imagine my mother not wanting me.

"She always wanted to be a singer. Like Loretta Lynn or Dolly Parton. One of those. You know. Get on the television, that's what she said she'd do. She used to sing with a band. She was real good too." The color came into Nell's face as she got going with her story. Her feet moved as if she were dancing, there in the muddy road.

"My ma's built exactly like Dolly Parton, you know. And her hair's the exact same color. From the back you couldn't tell 'em apart. You oughta hear her sing." Nell rolled her eyes. "If I put a blindfold on you, I bet you wouldn't be able to tell the difference between her and Dolly." She gave me a challenging look, daring me to disagree.

"I never heard her," I said, playing it safe. "And I never saw her either, so I can't really say."

"Once we were in a diner and this man came right up to her and asked her for her autograph. Thought she was Dolly Parton."

"That so?" I said in the way Maine people have when they don't want to commit themselves.

"Yeah, that's so." Nell mimicked me.

I peered down the hill, hoping the bus would come soon.

"You're some tough cookie," Nell said to me.

"I am?" I'd have to think about whether I liked that or not.

"We're a lot alike." Nell smiled at me so I knew her mood had changed and she was feeling friendly. I felt flattered when she said that. I don't know why, I just did.

"What makes you say that?" I asked her.

She shrugged. "In this life you watch out for *numero uno*. That's me. Number one. That's you too. You watch out for yourself. That's the only way to make it in this world. Be *numero uno* and you've got it made."

The bus finally came. As it bounced and swayed toward school, Nell's words kept going through my head. *Numero uno*. Number one. Watch out for yourself. We're a lot alike.

Was that true? I wondered. And if it was, was that good?

14

Rowena's mother changed her mind. She says we can't have her fur coat for our yard sale. Not if we're going to charge only two dollars for it. She's insulted, Rowena says. That coat was a present from her mother and father when she graduated from high school. It was very beautiful and cost a lot of money back then.

Even if it's old, it's worth more than two dollars, Rowena's mother says. You can't put a price on sentimental things, she says, and she's sentimental about that coat.

We asked Rowena what her mother thought was a fair price for her fur coat.

"Ten dollars," Rowena said, blushing. It wasn't her fault her mother changed her mind.

Nell snapped her fingers. "I got it!" she shouted. "We hang the fur coat out in front, so's the wind catches it, swings it back and forth. Everybody'll notice it then. It's a come-on. Lure the big spenders. They see it swaying there in the breeze from a distance, how do they know it's got the mange?"

"It does *not* have the mange," Rowena said indignantly. "You haven't even seen it. How do you know what it's got?"

"I figure your mother didn't graduate from high school yesterday," Nell said. Rowena got all red and opened her mouth, but before she could get herself worked up, Nell said, "Today's our dump day. My uncle says he's going there, he'll take us."

"Which uncle?" I asked her. I hoped it was the one with the spread out West and all the horses. It seemed to me he'd be more interesting than the one who drove the egg truck. But you never could tell.

Uncle Joe drove. He had kind of a nice face, all sort of red and bristly, and I liked his eyes, which were the size of dimes and very blue. He took the back way. We rode the ruts the winter had left in the road as if the pickup were a boat on stormy seas. Up and down, down and up we went. Uncle Joe sang to liven things up. "This old heap had a radio," he said, "I wouldn't bother. But I got to have music wherever I go." So he sang songs I'd never heard before, at the top of his lungs. He drove slowly so that Nell's brothers, trotting alongside, could keep up with the truck.

"They don't ride in cars if they can help it," Nell explained. "Makes 'em throw up. You ever been in a car with three people, all of 'em throwing up? All at the same time?"

I said no, I didn't think I ever had.

"It's fierce," Nell said. "Just plain fierce."

"I bet." I watched out of the corner of my eye as the brothers kept pace. They ran with frowning faces, chins and elbows tucked in, eyes straight ahead. Their concentration was terrific. They were in the Olympics. One of them was sure to win a gold medal. Their faces grew more and more flushed as I watched, until they looked like a trio of beets on legs. The littlest one kept losing ground. Even though his legs churned as fast as the other two, he kept dropping farther and farther behind until he was only a dot in the distance.

"Do your brothers have names?" I whispered to Nell. If they had, I'd never heard them. Betty and Rowena sat squinched together on the seat, rolling their eyes at us and Nell's uncle, keeping their traps shut for once. It was quite refreshing.

"Of course they have names," Nell said in a snippy voice. "Big guy's named Harold after my dad. Middle one's Leo. Little one's Eddie. Fast Eddie we call him on account of he's so slow."

I looked out the back window. Fast Eddie had disappeared. The other two kept on coming, although the truck was outdistancing them rapidly.

"Can he find his way back?" I wondered, meaning Fast Eddie. He was a small wisp of a boy with pale uneven eyes and thin pale hair that put me in mind of chicken fuzz. I'd never heard him say a word. He was in Tad's class at school. Tad allowed as how he'd never heard Fast Eddie say a word either, but that didn't prove anything. They'd make a fine pair, Fast Eddie and Tad. If they learned sign language they might be able to carry on a conversation.

"Oh, don't worry about him," Nell said. "He'll be right there, waiting for us on the way back."

The pickup pulled into the town dump. It was a bald, flat space at the end of a dirt road, surrounded on all sides by mounds of remains of people's lives. Piles of big black plastic garbage bags lined the roadway, spilling their contents haphazardly. Seagulls circled, eyeing the orange peels, eggshells, and coffee grounds, looking for a free meal. Three or four rats scuttled away as we hopped out of the pickup. Betty and Rowena let out a series of little piercing screams, but nobody paid any attention so they soon stopped.

Uncle Joe said he'd stay put. "You need help with anything," he told us, "just holler. I'm going to get some shut-eye."

"You take the left side," Nell directed us, "I'll take the right." I set off, Rowena and Betty bringing up the rear. "What're we looking for?" Betty said in an irritated way. Betty always got mad when she didn't have control of a situation. She hadn't wanted to come to the dump anyway. I'd made her. I'd told her she had to participate.

"What we want is nice big pieces of furniture we can fix up," I said. There were mounds of old tires, a few refrigerators without doors, a lot of auto parts, but no big pieces of furniture. Or small pieces, either, for that matter. No chiffoniers. The smell of burning rubber filled the air. Gulls squalled overhead, dipping, swooping, looking for good stuff too, maybe.

I saw two plastic garbage pails off to one side. They looked practically new. I ran over to claim them and discovered they were perfect except for each one having a big hole in its bottom. How'd those holes get there? I wondered. And how could they be patched up so the garbage pails would hold garbage?

"Look here!" Nell cried, stumbling toward us, carrying what looked like a rolled-up rug. Which is what it was. "You suppose somebody threw this away by mistake?"

"Maybe there's something inside," I said.

"Like what?"

"Maybe a person." I had heard that Cleopatra had herself rolled up in a rug so she could get to see Julius Caesar. That had always seemed very clever to me. I laid an ear to the rug and listened. It sounded empty.

"Stand guard," Nell said. "I got something else might be good." She darted behind a hill formed by a heap of discarded mattresses and came back lugging a two-wheel bike. Rusty, with bent wheels, and the paint peeling from it, it was a recognizable bike.

We stood in a semicircle, studying her latest find. "We can fix it up fine," we agreed. All things seemed possible.

When we were getting ready to load the stuff into the truck, Betty spied a lawn chair, its plastic webbing gone, leaning against a bulging trash bag. She whooped and hollered and carried on like she'd found buried treasure. Nell took one look, said, "That piece of junk!" with such scorn that we left the lawn chair where it was.

"What does she call that stuff *she* found?" Betty hissed, sending a shower of spit over us all. Uncle Joe woke, and we started back, keeping an eye out for the brothers. I figured Harold and Leo had each other. Fast Eddie was the one to worry about. We rounded a curve and there he was, lying on the side of the road, face lifted to the sky as if he were taking the sun at Popham Beach on the Fourth of July.

Nell rolled down the window and screeched, "Hey, pie face! Go back where you come from, why don'tcha?"

In a flash Eddie was on his feet, legs churning, making like a marathon runner. His rest had apparently done him good. Uncle Joe stopped the truck after a few minutes, called out, "Get in here before you bust something!" and Fast Eddie, winded at last, crawled in next to Rowena. I saw Rowena flinch and pull herself in tight, trying to put as much distance between herself and him as possible. But Eddie only breathed hard and stared moodily out the window, getting ready to throw up at any minute, until we pulled up in Nell's driveway. Fast Eddie was first out of the truck. He ran behind the house, and we heard sounds that told us he'd made it just in time.

15

I dreamed about my mother. Only she was my own age, a child with knobby knees and knobby elbows. She wore little white socks and black Mary Jane shoes and braces on her teeth. When she smiled, the sun caught in her braces and little lights flashed and danced in her mouth, blinding me. She had the most truly sparkly smile I'd ever seen. I dreamed that she and I were walking down a wide street with trees on either side so huge and wide their branches met, forming a canopy over our heads. I could smell the ocean. We held hands. Once in a while we skipped, but mostly we walked sedately, as if we were middle-aged.

And although we were exactly the same size and even wore matching dresses so that people passing us took us for twins, she acted much older. At every street crossing she looked both ways, then when the way was clear, she helped me across the street as if I'd just learned to walk and couldn't be expected to know the ways of the world.

I always dream in color. Some people I know dream in black-and-white. But in this dream the colors were very vivid. The sky and the grass and the flowers all were their true colors, only brighter than true colors, if you get my meaning. My mother's lips were rosy, and her hair was beautiful and shiny and long. I had never seen my mother with long hair in real life, only in photographs taken of her when she was a child. She kept calling me "my child," so that I laughed and said, "Don't call me that. I'm not your child."

At first there was no one in the dream except the two of us. Then, after a while, a crowd formed on the edges of the dream. It was a crowd of men and boys. They looked like Tad and Sidney and my father. It was amazing. We started to dance, my mother and I, and when we stopped, they clapped and whistled.

All of a sudden a big tall man appeared. He had on a wide-brimmed hat like the one my mother wears when she goes to Africa to photograph wild animals. Those hats are designed to keep the terrible African sun off your head. The stranger came up to us, tapped my mother on the shoulder and, next thing I knew, she had left me and was dancing with him. The crowd began to boo. The booing got louder and louder. The stranger and my mother stopped dancing. It was then I saw my mother was crying. Tears were streaming down her face, and she made no attempt to wipe them away. I pulled out a big handkerchief and went over to her. I offered her the handkerchief. She shook her head. Her face stayed wet. The tears splashed out of her eyes and flooded her cheeks.

I was alone. They had left me. All of them. My mother and I had turned into one and the same person. There I was, dressed in my black Mary Janes and my white socks, walking down the street under a canopy of trees. I smelled the ocean. I held hands with someone, but every time I turned to see whoever it was who was holding my hand, something came between us and I couldn't make out the person's face. Presently the sun went down and it was dark. I began to run. I ran and ran, trying to catch up. I was crying too. Just the way my mother had.

I woke up. I felt sad and mean, meaner than I ever had before. I hate dreams like that, the ones that begin so happily and end leaving such a dreadful empty feeling. At breakfast I took the biggest doughnut, the one with the most sugar on it. When Sidney said he wanted a glass of milk, I poured one for him although I was almost positive the milk was sour. I kept my head down and watched him as he drank it. He was halfway through before he made a face and said, "It tastes funny." I said, "Drink it and stop complaining," and he did. Then, to make up for it, I let him eat what was left of my doughnut.

"What's bothering you, Sky?" my father said after I'd slapped Tad's hand when he grabbed for something.

"Nothing," I snapped.

"You could've fooled me," he said. "You're not your usual sweet, adorable self." He reached over and patted my hand, and I jumped up.

"Sky's crying! Sky's crying!" Sidney shouted, rushing at me. "Aren't you crying, Sky? Aren't you?"

I pushed him. It wasn't a big push. Still, he went flying, skidding across the floor. He wasn't hurt. Only his pride.

"Did you hear from my mother yet?" I asked my father, knowing perfectly well if he had he would've told me. "Isn't it time for her to be coming home?"

"In the next couple of days we should get a cable," my father said, dusting Sidney off, telling me by his face and eyes that what I'd done wasn't nice. Which I already knew.

"Are you sure?" Sidney cried, hanging onto my father's leg.

And Tad, the man of few words, the realist, said, "Maybe."

Maybe what? Life was full of maybes, it seemed. Maybe my mother would come home soon. Maybe she'd be alone. Maybe she wouldn't. Maybe she'd bring Angus. Maybe she wouldn't. I'm sick to death of maybes.

I don't care, I told myself. If she wants to, she will. If she doesn't, she won't. It's as simple as that.

Ask anybody.

16

Next day a big moon-faced boy followed us home from the bus stop. I knew it was because Nell was walking with us. We were talking about having a knickknack table at our yard sale. Rowena and Betty discussed knickknacks in an easy way that indicated their familiarity with knickknacks. Last year my mother had gone through our house putting all our knickknacks into a box, which she donated to a thrift shop. She said they were nothing but dust catchers.

"I have this darling pin cushion that resembles a tomato," Betty said. "I also have some owl candles that have only been used once or twice that might be good." Rowena chimed in with the news that she had some salt and pepper shakers shaped like little fans that she thought would sell like hot cakes.

"We don't have any," Nell said in a tone that took care of any idea we had that she might add to our knickknack table.

What would we talk about when our yard sale was over? I wondered.

"Who *is* that creep?" Betty said, looking back over her shoulder, making sure the big moon-faced boy was still there. He was. He wore a baseball cap set backwards on his head, and a pair of gigantic wading boots that reached to his crotch. He kept spitting noisily to get Nell's attention.

"He's some dumb bozo," she said.

I was impressed by her use of the word "bozo." "He reminds me of Marlon Brando," I said.

Rowena came to a grinding halt in the middle of the road.

"What a terrible thing to say!" she shouted. Betty was so mad she wouldn't look at me. Even Nell took offense. They were all a little in love with Marlon Brando. Rowena and Betty had seen him in *On the Waterfront* on TV five times. I could take him or leave him alone.

"I can't help it," I said. "He does."

We went the rest of the way in silence. When we got to Nell's house, the moon-faced boy had disappeared. We unrolled the rug from the dump to inspect it. Nell's dog sniffed and lifted his leg tentatively.

"Take off, you old coot!" Nell hollered, kicking out at him. The dog skulked off a way and sat on his skinny rump, watching us.

No wonder he'd planned to pee on that rug. He figured he might as well join the crowd. Patches of dog pee made an elaborate design; big patches, little patches, medium-size patches. Plus it was some bald in spots, some raggedy in others.

"That should bring a fast five, ten cents," I said in a sour way. We stood looking down at our find, wondering what to do next. Nell's brother Leo stuck his head out the door and said, "Ma said to tell you you got to clean the kitchen today," he said.

"Clean it yourself," Nell told him.

"Ma says she might have to thump on you if you don't."

Nell tossed her curls, sending them to quivering like a bunch of bedsprings.

"Let's face it. If we're going to have a good yard sale, make some real money," she said, "we need more stuff to sell. We don't have nearly enough. We need a whole bunch of junk. The more the better. If we don't get ahold of more stuff, we better forget the whole thing.

It's not worth it with just the little bit of stuff we have now."

The three of us, Rowena, Betty, and I, stood meekly, listening to the general. We acted like our tongues had been cut out, not making a peep.

"Where do we get it?" Betty said. All eyes turned toward Nell. She was the leader, after all. She was the only one who knew what she was doing.

"First," she said, frowning, "we drive around some, take another trip to the dump, see what's laying around there. Maybe stop at some houses along the way, ask 'em if they have anything they want to get rid of that we can take off their hands. The ticket is"—Nell's foxy little face was excited, more excited than I'd ever seen it—"we give 'em a tax deduction for whatever they hand over. That gets 'em every time. That way they take off the value of what they donate to us off their income tax. You'd be amazed what telling them they get a tax deduction does to those folks. Why, they empty their attics and their cellars and everything else to get a tax deduction. It's like magic."

"How do we do that?" I said.

Nell spread her hands. "Simple as pie," she said. "We get ourselves a legal pad, one of those long yellow lined pads, makes it look very official and everything, and put in big letters at the top 'Tax Deduction.' Then we put their names on it, the date, and list the items they give us and their value. Price everything high, real high. That's important. That way, the more they give us, the more the tax deduction they get. And aim for the old folks. The older the better. The old people always have lots of stuff squirreled away in their houses. And they're all worried about money, getting sick and having to pay all those hospital bills and all, so if you tell 'em they get a big tax deduction for their things, they practically give you the shirt off their backs." Nell grinned. "I know because I did it. Plenty of times."

"That way," Rowena said, a smile breaking out on her face as she got the idea, "we help them, they help us. One hand washes the other."

"You got it," Nell said.

"What do they do with the tax deduction after we make it out and give it to them? What happens to it so they save money on their income tax?" I asked.

"They attach the piece of paper to their income tax returns and the government gives 'em the deduction next year. That way"—I was fascinated watching the way her tongue rolled around in her mouth—"that way they save piles of money."

I think I'd have known she was lying even if it hadn't been for her tongue. It was too easy. I'd watched my father make out his returns too many times, heard him complaining, seen him scratch his head, perplexed, as he tried to fill out the forms, to know it wasn't a simple problem to solve.

"Who'll drive us around? Your Uncle Joe?" Betty said.

"He's not here," Nell said. "I'll drive. If we stick to the back roads, we'll be all right."

"You're kidding," I said.

She gave me one of her flat stares. "No, I'm not," she said. "I know how to drive. Done it plenty of times, since I was about eight or nine. I know what I'm doing. It's not hard." She walked toward the old pickup parked in the driveway. "Who wants to come?"

Leo came to life. "I'll tell!" he hollered, jumping up and down, hitching up his trousers in a nervous way. Leo looks like he has a lot of bad dreams.

"No, you won't," Nell told him. "Not if you know what's good for you, you won't."

Leo subsided and sat on the edge of the bottom step, watching, his pale eyes slipping from side to side, seeing if anybody was going to try to stop her. Presently he put his finger up his nose and left it there, keeping it warm.

Nobody moved.

I stayed where I was, heard the truck engine start up, and watched as Nell drove around the corner of the house and stopped in front of us. I could see her perched on the edge of the seat so her feet could reach the gas pedal.

"See how I do it!" she cried, putting the truck in gear. She went forward, chugging and leaping, her head jerking back and forth like it might snap off.

"Hop in!" she shouted.

"Not me," Betty muttered. "Not on your life. My father'd have my hide."

Rowena nodded in wordless agreement. Nell gunned the engine, showing off. "You all are nothing but a bunch of scaredy cats!" she taunted.

Leo got up from his place on the steps and began pacing back and forth, his hands clasped behind his back, head down. The old dog came ambling from wherever it was he'd been sleeping. He was so thin I could see his ribs, count 'em, one by one. He had cataracts in both eyes and couldn't see too well, and he was deaf. Otherwise, he was in good shape, and I never saw a dog go after a bone like he did. He enjoyed eating and sleeping and chasing cars, and when strangers approached, he let out a resounding bark. I remembered that first day when we'd gone to welcome the new family and the way the dog had come to check us out, as if he owned the place. I liked him. He was a fine old gentleman.

Nell backed up, then put the car in forward gear and came at us. "Nothing to it!" she hollered. "Come on."

To my surprise, I said, "I'll go if you promise to drive on the back roads." Betty and Rowena stared at me. I don't know why I said I'd go. I guess I was showing off, too, the way Nell was.

Betty and Rowena linked arms and watched, their eyes big, as I climbed into the truck and sat beside Nell.

"You'll be sorry," I heard Betty say. We started up, tires squealing. Nell leaned into the steering wheel, sitting tall, turning that old wheel this way and that like she was driving one of Uncle Joe's mammoth egg trucks.

"How come you go backwards smooth as silk," I asked Nell, "but when you go forward, you jerk like to knock your head off?"

"Watch, just watch me." Nell put the truck into first. Slow and easy, she took her foot off the clutch and put it on the gas pedal. The truck went forward, as smooth as if it'd been oiled.

"See!" Nell crowed. "I told you I could do it. They'll wish they came with us. They're nothing but old feardy cats, that's what. Now hang on to your hat and we'll show 'em!"

Her foot slipped. I saw it slip off the brake and onto the gas. We zoomed forward, fast, faster than I would've believed possible for that old buggy to go. The engine made a terrible roar.

The old dog came at us. His lip was lifted, and I didn't know if he was smiling at us or snarling. The sound of a noisy car made him young again, I guess. I'd never know what made him spring at us. Maybe he thought we were trying to race him. Maybe he thought it was a game. He leaped up at us.

"Watch out!" I screamed. Nell jerked the wheel over hard, the way she'd seen Uncle Joe do. I felt a thud, a terrible thud against the truck's side. She jammed on the brakes. We sat there for a minute. Red spots darted in front of my eyes. Something or someone seemed to be doing somersaults inside my chest.

"I think you hit him," I said. Off to one side, I could see Betty and Rowena, their hands over their eyes, peering at us from between their spread fingers, the way you do when you watch a scary movie. Leo ran back and forth, waving his arms wildly, shouting, "You done it now! You done it now!"

The old dog lay, half under the left rear wheel, blinking at us. Stuff ran out of his mouth. He moaned, and the sound sent goose bumps up my spine. I jumped out and went over to him, bent down and touched his head. His tail thumped once and was still.

"Call the vet," I said. "Maybe he can . . ."

Nell squatted down beside me. "This old man's not going nowhere," she said. "What I gotta do is get this here truck off him and we'll see what's what." Even as she got back into the pickup and started the engine, I admired her cool. I couldn't imagine any situation in which Nell would get excited, cry or wring her hands,

107

the way people did, would lose her control. I shivered. The wind seemed to have risen, and as it sang its way through the dark pine forest ringing us around, a terrible pain glanced off one corner of my heart. Nell backed up smoothly, much more smoothly than she'd gone forward. The dog was free. There was nothing holding him now. Still he didn't move. I stood with my eyes shut, trembling.

Leo ran back and forth, shouting, thrusting his fists at the sky. Rowena and Betty put their arms around each other and touched foreheads. Nell and I stared down at the old dog. His eyes had rolled back in his head.

"I think he's dead," I whispered.

"Sure hope so," Nell said.

"What?"

"Sure hope so, I said. Doesn't look like he could be fixed up much. Now," she said briskly, "all's we got to do is get him out to the road." She took hold of one of the dog's legs and pulled. "Leo," she shouted over her shoulder, "go get the shovel." Leo brought it, and Nell and I worked the dog's body onto the shovel. Then we dragged it out to the road, where Nell upended the shovel and the body slid down and landed with a dull thump on the frozen road.

"What'd we do that for?" I asked. My head felt as if it were packed with cotton.

Nell stood back, surveying the scene. "That's good," she said, satisfied. "That way it looks like some car run over him. Hit-run. Happens all the time. Left him laying right there. That way we don't get blamed. They knew I was driving the truck, I'd get thrashed good."

"Is that why we brought him over here?" I asked, incredulous.

"Why'd you think?" Nell looked as me as if I were loony. "That's our story. And nobody's saying different. Right, Leo?" Leo crept behind us like an old man, moving back to his post on the porch, where he gazed out at the black pine trees with pale and desolate eyes.

Rowena and Betty swayed slightly, clutching each other, struck dumb.

"They'll never believe you," I said.

"Sure they will. All's I have to do is get the old pickup back to where it was." She got back in the truck and backed up until it was in pretty much the same spot it had been before.

"Now," Nell said, "I swear you to secrecy. Nobody's telling nothing, right? On account of they tell, I get it but good."

Leo's foot tapped a nervous rhythm on the step. He hummed off-key, keeping time with his foot.

"I'm going," I said. I walked out to look at the old dog. Maybe we were wrong. Maybe he was just resting and he'd be up and away in the morning. Maybe if I covered him with my jacket, he'd stay warm tonight. But looking at him, I knew it was no good. I touched him lightly in the little bony spot between his ears. He didn't stir.

It was no good at all.

"I'll tell you one thing, Nell Foster," I hollered. Rage made my voice strong. "I'm nothing like you. Not a bit! And don't say I am!"

17

As I cut across the field toward home, the wind pushed at me, trying to get me to turn back. I refused. I wouldn't go back there for anything. The salty air smelled good. So did the kitchen. Tonight my father had promised us a fried potato pigout. I wished I felt more like eating. My stomach wasn't itself. I saw the light in my father's study, which meant he was working. The boys were playing in their room. I could hear them moving furniture around. They are very big on moving their furniture around. My father says he suspects they'll grow up to be moving men.

I wanted to talk to someone about what had happened. There was no one. I had to sort out my feelings, get somebody else's opinion. I felt heavy, as if I'd eaten a huge meal. I sat in the big chair by the many-paned window my father had put in a few years ago—a wonderful spot to keep check on the weather and the wildlife that marches by outside. Once, when I was quite young, I got up very early and watched a whole family of deer, four of them, wander by, taking their time, checking out the joint. It was a thrill I'll never forget. In the winter when the snow is deep and there is a fresh coat of it every morning, the animal tracks left during the night make a weird and wonderful pattern. I have always found it soothing to sit there and look out. It's like a gigantic TV screen, featuring the wild creatures of the forest in living color. Very soothing.

Not today. My head teemed with images: the dog, Nell and her shovel, Leo waving his skinny arms and shouting. Me getting into the truck. Betty and Rowena watching, just watching.

What if the old dog had been a person? I couldn't get that thought out of my head. What if it'd been Leo or me or anyone else who'd been crushed under the truck's wheel? Would Nell have shoveled any one of us out into the road, stuff oozing out of our mouths, eyes fixed blindly on the gray sky? As bad as I felt, I had to give Nell credit. She sure was a quick thinker. That alibi of the hit-run driver had been right at her fingertips. Most people would've gone to pieces if they'd hit and killed a dog. Not her. She'd never lost her cool. And that dog had been her friend.

I heard a car pull up outside. Oh, Lord. I wiped my face on my sleeve and had almost made it out of the room when Pamela came in, hugging herself, saying, "It's cold." The last person in the world I needed right then was Pamela.

"Hi, Sky," she said in her usual brittle manner. Then she took one look at me and said, "Something wrong?"

That did it. I started to cry and, once started, I couldn't stop. I didn't want to cry in front of her. There was nothing I could do about it. The tears kept coming. Silently she handed me a handkerchief and sat down, saying nothing. I did appreciate that. I really did. I blew my nose.

Still she said nothing. I think if she'd said, "Can I help?" or "What's wrong?" I would've run and hidden under my bed. But because she had the good sense to keep quiet, I found myself sitting down next to her and telling her what had happened.

I told her the whole story, about how I'd been in the truck with a friend driving—I didn't name any names— and we'd hit the friend's dog and killed him. Then—and this was harder, much harder to say—I told her about the friend getting out, checking the dog to see if he was dead, then pulling him by his leg.

"Then she called to her brother, 'Go get the shovel,'" I told Pamela, "and they got him onto it and dragged the shovel out to the road and dumped the dog there." A shudder ran over me. I heard Pamela catch her breath.

"She told us we weren't to tell anyone because if we did she'd get it but good," I said. "She said if anyone wanted to know what had happened, we were supposed to say the dog must've been killed by a hit-run driver."

There was a scuffling sound in the hall. I heard Tad say, "It's her!" and then the sound of running feet as they scurried back to move some more furniture.

"And you know something?" I said in a loud voice. Pamela waited quietly for what I would say.

"She never showed any signs of remorse, the way they always say after somebody commits a crime," I said. "She never even bent down to see if he was alive or dead. She never said, 'I'm sorry,' or anything. She just loaded him onto that shovel and dragged him out and dumped him like he was a sack of meal. I never saw anything like it. It was like something she did every day of her life. She didn't think twice."

I got up and went to the kitchen for a paper towel to blow my nose on. I'd used up all the dry spots on Pamela's handkerchief. "The worst of it is," I said, "is I

114

feel guilty. Maybe if I hadn't been in the truck it never would've happened. If I hadn't said I'd go with her, maybe she wouldn't have gone either. I egged her on. I know I did. So I'm partly responsible." I hoped Pamela would say, "No, no, of course you're not," but she didn't. She nodded slightly, and I felt she was agreeing with me. I *was* partly responsible for what had happened.

"I don't know if I should tell on her. Do you think I should?" I asked Pamela. If someone had told me yesterday that today I'd be asking her for advice, I would've told them they had rocks in their head. But now I needed advice.

"Would it do any good to tell on her?" Pamela said. "Would it accomplish anything?"

I thought about that. "I don't know," I finally said. "Her mother would probably beat the daylights out of her. That's what she said anyway."

I thought some more. "As far as bringing the dog back or making her promise she'd never do anything like that again, it wouldn't accomplish much, that's for sure. It wouldn't make her sorry for what she'd done. I don't think she'd ever be sorry. Because she doesn't think she did anything wrong." As soon as the words were out, I realized that was the truth. *Nell didn't think she'd done anything wrong.* Fantastic.

Pamela got up, and I realized she was still wearing her coat. "I'll tell you what," she said. "Why don't you sleep on what you told me, and tomorrow, if you get a chance, talk it over with your father. See what he thinks. That might be the best thing to do."

"All right," I said, glad of any adult advice. "I'll do that."

Pamela opened the door to the mud room.

"Aren't you staying for supper?" I asked.

"Not tonight. Tonight you'll all do better without me. Maybe tomorrow. Sleep on it, Sky. It's always a good idea to sleep on something like that. Sometimes it helps."

I ran to the door. She was already halfway down the path.

"Thanks," I called out. "Thanks a lot."

She lifted a hand in good-bye and took off down the hill. I went back inside, set the table, and thought about her. So that's Pamela, I said to myself. You were wrong about her. She's not so bad, after all.

18

My mother came home that night. My father was la-
dling out potatoes when she came. She stood in the
doorway, smiling at us.

"Here I am," she said. She was alone.

For one second the only sound in the room was the
fat burbling in the frying pan, making noises like a baby
discovering its toes and fingers for the first time. My
father stood at the stove. Sidney slid down in his chair
and dug his fists into his eyes the way he does when
he's overcome. Tad overturned the bottle of ketchup he

was holding, and we watched it run out into a widening pool on the table.

I was the first to recover. I ran to her and hugged her. The boys came to life and clambered over my mother as if she were a jungle gym. They grabbed at bits and pieces of her, each trying for the lion's share.

"Stop, stop!" she cried joyfully.

We danced around the room, hopping, skipping, shouting out in pleasure. Only my father stood apart, smiling slightly, holding his plate.

"Why didn't you call?" he said at last in a hoarse voice. "You said you would."

"I got in earlier than I expected, and there was a rental car someone had just turned in so I took it, and here I am." She went over to him and brushed his cheek with her lips. "Aren't you glad to see me?"

"Sky," my father said, "get a plate for your mother. We better eat these while they're hot. We're having a potato pigout, Mary."

"Perfect. I'm starving." We all sat down, and for a few minutes nobody said anything. Then we all started talking at once.

"Fill me in on what's been happening here," my mother said.

"Nothing! Nothing's been happening!" the boys shouted.

"Life went on as usual," my father said.

118

"Sky," my mother said, "you look so pretty." I flushed. I could feel myself flush. She was being nice because she'd been away and was glad to be back.

The boys stopped climbing on her and sat still, looking at me, studying my face. Sidney screwed up his face so he looked like a little old man. Or a baby chimp is more like it. He tilted his head to one side and said, "Sky looks pretty?" a question mark tacked on the end.

Tad chewed slowly, squinting at me. " 'Course," he said in a grown-up, superior way, "she always looks pretty."

It was almost more than I could bear.

After a while my mother looked at her watch and said, "It's bedtime, way past bedtime for you two." She took each boy by his hand.

"Daddy, you come too," they shouted. "You come too!" They figured if they got enough people together they could have a party and put bedtime off ever further. I know those two. They're operators.

"How about the presents?" Sidney said.

"When I unpack tomorrow, not now," she answered.

"Not tonight," my father said. "It's your mother's turn." I went with her. The room smelled of Tad and Sidney and their unwashed socks, which were hidden around the room like eggs at an Easter egg hunt. They were supposed to put them in the hamper, but I knew if I made a search, I'd find enough dirty socks tucked away in corners to outfit an octopus.

My mother read them a story, a short one. I listened, pretending I was a child again. The boys horsed around some more, and my mother finally said, "That's enough," in a way that made them know she meant what she said. We tucked them in and went back to the living room. My father stood where we'd left him. He didn't seem to have moved. My father is a true artist at standing still. He does it with such ease, never making small talk or needless gestures. He stands still while others work themselves into a flurry, and presently his stillness takes over. I'd seen it happen, and now it was happening again.

"Well," my mother said. "It's good to be home." She put her arm around me. "Did you miss me?" she said.

"A little." In the morning I'd tell her how much, tell her everything. Right now I was tired. Very tired. My mother yawned.

My father discarded his stillness as if it were a cape. He went to my mother and put his hands on her shoulders.

"I'm glad you made it back safely, Mary," he said.

She leaned against him for a moment. I saw her. She must be very tired, I thought, to do that. Then she reached up to him and kissed him. I saw her. I couldn't believe my eyes. I thought they'd given up kissing. Nobody seemed to be giving me the time of day. I didn't care. I said good night and went to bed. I lay there, wondering what had happened to the great white hunter. And thinking it was a good thing Pamela had left when she had. And I planned what I'd say in the morning. I liked the sound of their voices rising and falling.

I'd tell them in the morning about the old dog. I wanted to get it off my chest now, this minute, but I knew if I did, I might start bawling again, and I didn't want to spoil my mother's homecoming.

19

"*The boys are still asleep,*" *my mother said when I came* to breakfast. "They're basket cases after last night. I thought you would be too. What would you like?"

I drank my juice. "Just a piece of toast, please."

"And some cereal. You need a good breakfast to think straight," she told me. How many times have I heard her say that? I wish a good breakfast *was* all I needed to make me think straight.

"Tell me about the family in the Johnsons' house," my mother said, putting the butter on the table. "How's the new girl? Have you made friends with her?"

"She's O.K.," I said. "Kind of different."

"Oh?" My mother gave me her full attention. Different people always interested her. "In what way?"

"Crocuses are up," my father said from where he stood at the window.

"High time." My mother went to stand next to him, and I noticed she put her hand on his shoulder.

"Something terrible happened yesterday," I blurted out.

They turned toward me, their faces sympathetic and apprehensive.

"Nell's dog got killed."

"How?"

I told them. I hadn't meant to, but I did. I told them everything. It didn't take me long. I was surprised. I'd thought it would take a lot longer than it did.

"The bad part was," I told them, winding down, "she wasn't sorry. She didn't think what she'd done was wrong. That's what really got me. She didn't care."

"Poor Sky." My mother's eyes were wet. "It's awful when someone you like and trust disappoints you, isn't it?"

I didn't exactly like Nell, I thought. And I never even thought about whether I trusted her or not. She was exciting. She wasn't like anybody I'd ever known before. I thought it was wonderful to know somebody like her because she was so different.

"Not much you can do, I'm afraid," my father said. "Except next time somebody tries to talk you into doing something you know is wrong, resist temptation. Maybe if you hadn't agreed to get in the truck, Nell wouldn't have actually driven it."

That was true. I'd said as much to Pamela but not to my mother and father.

My father patted me on the head. "It builds character to resist temptation, Sky. Did you know that? And character may be an old-fashioned virtue, but it never goes out of style. I've got to get to work. Good-bye," and he left the room.

"What happened to Angus?" I said. I'd been wanting to ask my mother, but I'd waited until my father wasn't around. "Why didn't he come with you?"

"It didn't work out," she said. "It turned out that Angus already had a perfectly good wife and children back home in Australia. He just neglected to tell me. And I thought he was different and wonderful to know too, just as you felt about Nell. And he was."

"Poor Mom," I said to her. "I've gotta go, or I'll miss the bus. See you, Mom," and I bent to kiss her. "I'm glad you're home."

"So am I," she said.

When I got to the bus stop, Nell was already there, talking to the Kimball girls and Jerry and Ollie Brown, telling them some tale that had them goggle-eyed. Lord knows what she was telling them.

I marched right up to her.

"What'd your mother say?" I said.

"About what?"

"About the dog."

"Oh," she said airily, "some car smacked him up good. One of those hit-run drivers, most likely. Harold found him laying in the road. We lugged him out to the woods." She ran her hand over her curls, caressing them.

"Poor old coot. Never knew what hit him." She smiled at me, and her chipped tooth gave her face a carefree air.

I looked at her, wordless. Leo hid behind Fast Eddie. He refused to look at me.

"My mother got home from Africa last night," I said.

"My uncle's driving his truck all the way to Rhode Island," she said back.

"You hear what I said?" I snapped.

"You hear what I said?" A smile shaped itself around her mouth, missing her eyes. "Plenty of people go to Africa," she said. "Come back, too. You think it's so hotsy-totsy your mother went and come back. It's nothing so big."

The Kimball girls and Ollie and Jerry Brown giggled.

"You're full of garbage, you know that? You don't even

try to be nice. You're just full of garbage." I turned my back on her. I was so mad I was afraid I'd cry.

I could heard her stealthy steps as she crept up behind me. "Want me to tell you how I make their tongues tingle?" she whispered, so close I could smell her musty smell.

"No," I lied.

" 'Course you do. It's my secret way my mother handed down. Her mother told her and her mother's mother before that. They were gypsies. Only gypsies know how to make their tongues tingle. It's an ancient secret handed down over the centuries."

I was tempted to turn and face her down, say, "All right. Tell me how to make their tongues tingle." But I knew if I did, I would be in her power. So I stayed where I was, looking out over the snow-covered fields, watching the gulls wheel overhead, crying their hoarse cries. I heard the bus rumbling up the hill. It was my last chance. If I asked her now, she would still tell me. But I held on, gritting my teeth, and didn't ask. Like my father said, resisting temptation builds character. And when the bus pulled up and Bill swung open the door, I got on and sat next to Saralou Hunkle, who was in my second and third grade classes until somebody discovered she was practically a genius and she skipped a couple of grades and now she plans on being a chemical engineer.

"Hi," I said. Saralou raised her head from her textbook and gave me one of the groggy stares she specializes in. She wasn't sure she knew who I was, but she was going to give me the benefit of the doubt.

"Oh, hi," she said. "How're things?" Saralou Hunkle was a barrel of laughs.

I felt a finger in the middle of my back. I turned. Nell laughed and said, "You missed your chance. I'll never tell you now."

"What's she talking about?" Saralou asked me.

I shrugged. "I don't know. She's loco." Already I was sorry I'd sat next to Saralou, sorry I hadn't said, "All right, then, how do you make their tongues tingle?" But it was too late.

Behind me, Nell thumped her knees against the back of my seat. It drove me crazy, but I didn't let on. She wasn't going to get my goat.

"You want to come over Saturday?" Saralou said. Before I had a chance to answer her, Nell leaned forward and said, "She can't."

"Mind your own business!" I cried.

Nell flashed her chipped-tooth smile at me. "We got to plan the yard sale. Those girls said we have to plan all day Saturday." She always calls Rowena and Betty "those girls," as if they didn't have any names.

"They didn't say anything to me about it," I said, sitting stiff and formal next to Saralou, who collapsed back into her book and lost interest in me. Maybe she couldn't remember who I was, after all. I couldn't blame her. Sometimes I had a tough time remembering who I was myself.

When we got to school and Bill let us out, he said, "Thaw's coming. I can smell it. Early this year. Good thing too. I had enough of winter. How about you?"

"You said it," I agreed. I hoped he was right. I wasn't watching where I was going and stepped into a giant mud puddle. I could feel the mud seeping into my boot.

"Watch where you're going!" Nell called out, laughing. "You hafta keep your eyes open in this world, you wanta get ahead."

Without looking at her, I went inside, the mud squelching damply inside my sock the whole way.

All right for you. I didn't believe her for one minute about her mother being a gypsy. I just plain didn't believe her.

Besides, who ever heard of a blond gypsy? There's no such thing. All gypsies have black hair. Ask anybody.

20

Betty's grandmother died last winter over in Waldo-boro. Her mother's clearing out the house, getting rid of things. She says we can have the collection of Betty's grandmother's hats she found in the attic. About twenty-five or thirty of them, she says, and each one more of a conversation piece than the other. Betty's father plans on driving up there in his big old station wagon that gets about fifteen miles to the gallon. Still, it's cheaper than renting a U-Haul, he says, and just as commodious. Betty also plans to set up a table of her best-sellers, the ones she's through with. She's going to give each prospective buyer a little rundown on the plot so they'll know what they're in for. How to kill sales is what I call it.

Bill, the bus driver, was right. Spring seems to have come early this year. The mud season is here. But the sun is actually warm, and my father has planted his peas and lettuce—always a good sign.

We're busy drawing posters for the yard sale. We're putting those posters every place we can think of: the post office, the gas station, the general store, the library. All the posters give the date and time and place and say in big black letters: NO EARLY BIRDS. That was Nell's idea. She said people are so eager to get bargains they start lining up at sunrise. So NO EARLY BIRDS means what it says. If anyone cares.

Maybe we'll make some money, after all. We told the minister's wife if we did we'd donate something to the church. That was after she gave us a set of dishes she couldn't stand. She said she'd used those dishes for twenty years, hating every minute of it. I can understand why, too. They're made of fat china, the most horrible mustardy color you ever saw. Still, one man's meat is another man's poison, as they say, and somebody may fall in love with those fat dishes. It's doubtful, but you never can tell.

We included a snow date on our posters. I hope we

don't have to use it. Everyone will fall apart if we do. It would be such an anticlimax. Nell drew up a diagram of where each of us should set up our card tables. She's very businesslike and directs us like a general planning a battle. I haven't really talked to her since she told me her mother was a gypsy. One day last week I was downtown and I hung around the Down East Beauty Salon, where Mrs. Foster works, hoping for a glimpse of her. But it was a day they stay open late, and she never showed. I didn't dare go inside. I was afraid they might ask me if I wanted a wash and set and maybe even a manicure. I was afraid they might pop me under the dryer before I could protest, and then what would I do?

Rowena asked our teacher if we could put up a poster in our home room. She said once that started everyone would want to put up a poster advertising something or other. It was Betty's idea to put one up down at the bus station. The next day we went down to see how it looked and it was already gone. Someone had ripped it off. I couldn't believe it. None of us could. Only two buses a day, and already someone had torn down our sign. It's enough to make you lose your faith in human nature.

It turns out Rowena's mother's changed her mind again. She says we can have her fur coat for the sale if we price it at eight fifty. And not a penny less. We took a vote on it. I voted for it, and so did Rowena and Betty. Nell was the only holdout. She said the coat wouldn't bring a cent more than five dollars. We over-ruled her. Nell doesn't take to defeat. I walked home with her after our meeting, and she sulked all the way.

Rowena's mother wants half of the eight fifty. If we sell her coat for that much. She wants fifty percent commission. She told Rowena to tell us that. Poor Rowena.

Nell hasn't said anything more about getting old folks to give us stuff from their attics and we give 'em a tax deduction in return. I asked my father about that, and he said he didn't think it sounded right. Only estab-lished charities you give donations to, he said, can give you a tax deduction on the things you give. Good old Nell. She sure does try. Give her that.

"The kid sounds like a first-class charlatan," my fa-ther said, shaking his head. I thought it was in admi-ration, but I couldn't be sure. "If she doesn't get to be chairman of the board, she'll probably wind up behind bars."

21

The morning of the yard sale dawned foggy but with patches of blue showing out over the water. I felt groggy and cross, like a baby waking from a nap. I snuck out of the house early, so the boys wouldn't follow me. I didn't want them over at Nell's yet.

Mrs. Sykes was already there, perched behind the wheel of her car, looking like a hen on its roost. It was possible she'd spent the night in Nell's yard. I wouldn't put it past her.

"What kept you?" she said in her grouchy way. "I

been here for hours. When's this fool sale start? I'm on the lookout for bargains. Never pay full price for anything, my husband always said. He was right, too."

I pointed out the "NO EARLY BIRDS" warning. She brushed me off as if I'd been a mayfly.

"If they weren't outa staters"—she jerked a thumb in the direction of Nell's house—"they'd be up and about now like good country folk should. They're slugabeds."

A curtain in one of the downstairs rooms stirred, and a pale, murky face looked out at us. They were up and about, outa staters or no. I set up my card table in the yard and arranged some stuff my mother had given me when she'd been seized with one of her clearing-out fits. A half-empty bottle of perfume, a box of dusting powder that hadn't even been opened, a picture frame encrusted with shells, and a calendar that said "World's Fair 1939." Treasures, all.

Another car pulled up. A man leaned out and shouted, "This the place?" Before I even had a chance to answer, the car doors opened and people spilled out, the way clowns in the circus tumble endlessly from one of those tiny cars. They milled about, inspecting my goods. "Where's the good stuff?" they said. "This is mostly junk." I tried not to have hurt feelings, even though I knew that what they said was halfway true.

"It doesn't start until nine," I said in a feeble voice. The man slapped a large, grimy hand down on my table and said, "This ain't hardly worth the price of the gas it took getting here," looking at me from under heavy crusted eyelids. I knew if I said again that the sale didn't start until nine, he wouldn't listen, so I said nothing and watched them pile back into the car and roar down the road. Two more cars appeared, spewing forth prospective customers. I had to turn them all away. After they'd made insulting remarks about my offerings, that is. Still no sign of Rowena or Betty or Nell. Where was she? She must know all these people were showing up in her front yard. Why didn't she come out and help me?

In the meantime Mrs. Sykes had snuggled down in her back seat, covering herself with an afghan she said she'd knitted herself, bidding me to wake her when the action started.

I was about to give up, go back home and eat breakfast until it got close to nine. Then I saw Rowena looming over the horizon, dragging her card table. Her mother followed, dressed in her print dress and her black shoes with the heels. I looked to see if she was carrying some of her bread. Instead, her arms were filled with a large white box that she carried with tender, loving care, as if it were a newborn baby about to be christened. I went to help them, glad to have something to do.

Rowena's mother shrugged off my offers of help and insisted on carrying her burden into Nell's yard, right up to the porch. She laid it down, smiled at us, and removed the cover slowly.

"Now," she said, "if someone could fetch me a hanger."

As if she'd been listening at the front door, Nell appeared, rubbing her eyes. "I just woke up," she said.

I looked at her hard. "You did not," I said. "I saw you at the window fifteen minutes ago. Lots of people been here already and gone. Probably won't come back. I was here all alone. I could've used some help."

"If I could have a hanger upon which to hang my coat," Rowena's mother said snootily, speaking to the sky, "it would be most appreciated."

"I'll see if we got an old one we can spare," Nell said in a loud voice. "A real old one." She went back into the house, and Rowena and I spent some time setting up her card table. Nell returned with an old wire hanger, and Rowena's mother made a ceremony out of removing her fur coat from the box and arranging it on its hanger with loving, gentle hands. So as not to bruise the fur, I guess.

"Where is the best place," she inquired in her company voice, "for us to display the merchandise?"

Nell snatched the coat from her. "Here," she said, leaping, agile as a cat, onto the porch railing and hanging the coat from a large hook suspended from the ceiling. "There," Nell said, brushing the palms of her hands together, "that's good. Nothing can happen to it up there. Everyone'll see that old coat right when they pull up. They can't miss seeing it."

Rowena's mother, torn between pleasure at the high visibility of her prize and dismay at hearing it referred to as "that old coat," seemed unsure what to do now.

"Why don't you go on home?" Rowena suggested with a bright smile. "It'll be a while yet before business starts to boom."

"I believe I will. I will return, however, to help in any way I can," she said, and we watched her leave.

Nell's brothers appeared, large and looming, the way good yard sale guards should look, and stood, arms folded across their chests, ready to do battle with any thieves. Even Fast Eddie, suited up for the occasion in what were obviously hand-me-down clothes, too large, too billowing for his small frame, stood, wispy and unafraid and glowering. It was a good family turnout.

I finally got to see Nell's mother. She passed by in the car. Uncle Joe was driving. She was looking at herself in a little mirror, fixing her hair, patting it. She looked up just for a second, right at me. She didn't smile. I didn't think she looked *that* much like Dolly Parton. I mean, I don't think I would've asked her for her autograph the way Nell said the man in the diner had. She was blond, very blond, but that was about it. Of course, I didn't hear her sing. But Dolly has a sweet face. From what I could see of Nell's mother, her face wasn't sweet. It was sort of hard.

Nell said importantly, "She has a nine o'clock perm plus a manicure." I wished I'd had a better look at her.

Mrs. Sykes woke up and hopped out of her car, and when she caught sight of Rowena's mother's fur coat dangling from its hook, swaying in the wind, she demanded to try it on. Anyone could see that Mrs. Sykes would swim in that coat. Still, she insisted, so Nell took it down from its ceiling hook.

When Mrs. Sykes put it on, it looked as if she'd draped a bear rug over herself. No one was rude enough or had courage enough to laugh, but she was a comical sight in that coat.

"Name your price," Mrs. Sykes said, plainly pleased with herself. When Rowena said, in a timid voice, "Eight dollars and fifty cents," Mrs. Sykes yelped like a scalded cat and let out a roar that could be heard for a mile. "Eight dollars and fifty cents!" she hollered. "Not mink, is it? Looks like good old raccoon to me. By gory, you folks are bandits, pure and simple. Nothing but bandits! I'll give you two dollars for it. Not a penny more. All it's worth is two dollars. Tops. That's my top price."

We told her Rowena's mother wouldn't take a cent less. Mrs. Sykes then refused to take off the coat and wandered around, getting the feel of it, as she said. Betty's mother and father arrived with their laden-down station wagon, carrying all of Betty's grandmother's hats plus other stuff from her attic. They added a great deal to the yard sale, I will say. We stood around and watched as the hats were taken out of their boxes and displayed. There were a number of black hats that looked like platters and/or coal scuttles. Then there was a bright green one that Betty's mother said her mother had worn every St. Patrick's Day, although she didn't have a drop of Irish blood in her. There were hats with feathers and hats without. But Mrs. Sykes found her heart's desire in a purple plush hat that was too big for her, like the fur coat, and fell down around her head and ears, obscuring most of her face.

She was a picture.

Cars kept arriving, pulling up in the muddy road, disgorging passengers. Several people got as far as the front door of Nell's house and were stopped, hands on the doorknob, looking for genuine antiques that might be hidden inside. Either that or the bathroom. Or food. Coffee and doughnuts were what they wanted. We sent them down to the village for that, to their dismay. Business was brisk, prices low. I sold my stuff in half an hour. Several offers were made on the fur coat after Mrs. Sykes took it off. The highest bid was four seventy-five. Rowena's mother heard that and almost fainted. Betty had a ball telling the plots of all her best-sellers. One woman leaned her elbow on the table and kept saying, "And then what happened?"

Mrs. Sykes bought the purple hat, plus a baby blue one. We let her have both for a dollar, and that set her up some. Business was so good we decided to hold the sale over one day. Everyone agreed to run home and see what else they could get from their attics. The minister's wife's fat dishes went to a young couple who told us they were about to be married. We let them have them for a song.

Nell kept all the money in an old cigar box. We handed in our receipts at the end of the day and sat around counting it. There was a total of twenty-five dollars and ten cents. No one knew where the odd ten cents came from. My mother brought the boys over and let them each buy one thing. Tad bought a bag full of marbles for a nickel, and Sidney chose a used baseball bat and glove for a dime. They went away, satisfied.

Having a yard sale is exhausting. That I know. At the end of the day we were all tired. But it had been worth it. Tomorrow would be better. Nell said she'd keep Rowena's mother's coat in a safe place for the night. Rowena's mother came sniffing around and said she thought Mrs. Sykes had worn her coat. But she wanted to hold out for the eight fifty. She kept saying how much that coat meant to her. I guess it did mean a lot. More than two dollars, anyway.

22

Tad's second tooth is hanging by a thread. He's guarding it with his life. He walks around with his hand over his mouth so Sidney won't see how loose it is. Sidney wrote a letter to the tooth fairy. I helped him with the spelling. The note says, "KEEP OUT." Sidney says he's going to tape the note to the bedroom door so the tooth fairy will see it. Tad says if Sidney does that, he's going to get it.

My mother said she'd set up a cot in her room, and Sidney can sleep there until the tooth falls out and Tad collects from the tooth fairy. Sidney says O.K. That suits him. He still wants to put the note on the door, but we won't let him.

My mother brought us all African bush hats for presents. They are very soft and wide-brimmed, and they have a chin strap to keep them on. I think they're elegant. I could tell the boys were disappointed that they didn't get what they asked for, but she said she wasn't able to bring out live animals or animal tusks, that the customs officials said it was against the law. My mother says she doesn't think she'll be going back to Africa for a long time. She says she's going up to northern Maine to shoot some pictures of moose for a magazine. Moose are unique animals, as unique in their own way as rhinos and hippos. She plans to stick around for a long time, she says.

"The boys'll be glad," I told her. "So will I. And so will Dad. We missed you something awful."

"Sky," she said, laughing, "you never quit, do you?"

I told my mother about finding the old chair up in the attic and how I'd wanted to have it for the yard sale and Dad wouldn't let me. I repeated the story he'd told us about the history of the chair and why he wanted to keep it. She listened intently, her face flushed. When I'd finished, she didn't say anything. Once or twice she ran her hand over her hair to smooth it. After, I was glad I'd told her that story. It might make a difference.

It was a tender, touching story, a story any woman would like to hear, it seemed to me.

"Speaking of the yard sale, how'd it go today?" she asked me. "Did you make a lot of money?"

"It was very successful. We made twenty-five dollars and ten cents. As a matter of fact," I said, "it was so successful we put up more signs and we're going to have it again tomorrow. Do you have anything else you could give me to sell?"

"I might have. I'll see. Did you sell the fur coat?"

"Not yet. Rowena's mother's holding out for eight dollars and fifty cents. Mrs. Sykes wants it for two dollars, and another lady offered four dollars and seventy-five cents."

"Well, maybe they can reach a compromise," my mother said.

"She's very sentimental about that coat," I said.

"Yes," my mother said solemnly. "I can see that."

Next day I overslept. I could tell by the way the light hit the foot of my bed that it was late, probably past eight. I better hotfoot it over to Nell's to arrange the goods, set out the costume jewelry my mother had given me last night. It was extremely nice costume jewelry and should bring a good price. There was a necklace with green and red stones in it and matching earrings. Plus an almost silver bracelet. It wasn't sterling silver, but if you didn't look close, you couldn't tell. I pulled on my old clothes and grabbed a handful of cold cereal and a piece of bread to eat on my way.

The place looked deserted. The old pickup truck was gone, I noticed, and when I finally knocked on the door, there was no sound from inside. I looked in the windows at last and could see no people. I knocked again, really hard this time, and waited for someone to fling open the door. Maybe they'd all overslept too.

I went around to the back. There were lots of tire marks left in the soft ground, and a couple of boxes filled with paper and cans and bottles. I tried the back door and, to my amazement, it swung open. I stepped in and hollered, "Anybody here?"

The house rang with silence. You know how you can tell there's nobody in a house? There's a certain stillness to it. I thought Nell and her brothers might be pulling a joke, might be hiding behind the door to jump out at me. I closed the back door with a big crash so if somebody was upstairs they'd know I was there.

"Hey!" I cried, "it's me, Schuyler Sweet. It's almost time for the sale to start." If Nell's mother was upstairs, she'd never met me and she'd think I was a burglar. I walked into the hall and called again. There were some chairs and a table or two in the living room. Not much furniture. It belonged to Mr. Johnson, Nell had told me. They'd brought some things of their own, but most of the furniture was his. The place was very messy. In the kitchen were dirty plates and an overturned can of beer. I opened the refrigerator—I don't know why, but I did. Inside was a bottle of sour milk and a half-used bottle of club soda. That was all.

I couldn't figure out where they were. Suddenly a terrible thought struck me. Maybe they'd been murdered. The whole family wiped out. I'm always reading stories in the newspapers about whole families being murdered. A cold hand ran down my spine. I inched my way toward the back door. Slowly, quietly, so if the murderer was still upstairs, he wouldn't hear me. I was frightened. The only thought in my head was to get out of there. And fast. I ran to my house and told my father, and he came back with me to Nell's house.

He and I went inside and I followed him upstairs. The rooms were empty. I kept my eyes half closed so that if there were bodies and blood I wouldn't see everything. My father called and hollered and still nobody came.

"They've gone," my father said. "They've skinned out, it would seem."

"Skinned out?" I said. "What do you mean? We're having the yard sale today. How could they have skinned out?"

"I don't know," he said. "But that's the way it looks. Unless they're all at church."

"That's a possibility," I said. "I didn't think they went

to church, but we better wait. If they're there, they'll be home soon."

We went back home to wait. I sat by our kitchen window, from which I could just see Nell's driveway and the front porch. If they came, I could see them drive up. But no one came. Until Rowena and Betty arrived. I ran out and called to them, and they came over and climbed the fence that separated our yards.

When I told them the house was empty and we were waiting to see if the Foster family came home from church or wherever they'd been, Rowena asked in a sharp voice, "Where's my mother's fur coat?"

"Oh, my gosh," I said. "I don't know."

"If it's gone," Rowena said, "she'll kill me."

"Why would it be gone?" I said. "What a ridiculous idea. It can't be gone."

"Then where is it? You said you went through the house, and it wasn't there. Did you check the closets?"

"No," I said. "I didn't." We waited some more. Several cars pulled up and people got out. We could see them walking around the house, wondering where the yard sale was. We didn't go over. My father said it'd be better if we sat tight for a while. There was probably some simple explanation, he told us, for their whereabouts.

We waited a long time. We saw a man drive up in a truck, get out and try the front door. Then he went around back. He must've gone inside. After a while he came out, looked up at the house and shook his fist at it. He drove down the road and stopped at our house. My father went to the door. It was Mr. Johnson, the man who owned the house. He was looking for the Fosters, he told us. They were behind in their rent and he'd come to collect. We said we didn't know where they were.

Rowena's mother came up the road at a gallop. Rowena said, "I better go see what she wants." She went out, trembling. We watched Rowena's mother wave her arms about, then turn and stomp off.

"Maybe they got in an auto accident," Betty said. "Maybe they're all in the hospital."

We waited a little longer. Nobody came to the house except people looking for the yard sale. I thought of the twenty-five dollars and ten cents Nell had with her in the cigar box. I thought of Nell's brothers hurtling through the State of Maine in Uncle Joe's pickup, maybe throwing up all over the back seat right at this minute. I tried to imagine Nell's mother belting out one of Dolly Parton's songs in a lighthearted fashion, sitting beside Uncle Joe, wearing Rowena's mother's fur coat to keep her warm.

I thought of the old dog.

When I couldn't sit still another minute, I told Betty and Rowena I was going for a walk in the woods.

"What for?" they asked me. "You think they're hiding out there?" Rowena's mother had gone home, threatening to call the police. She was in a state. She was going to sue somebody, she said. I don't know who.

"They're far away by now," I said. "I just want to take a walk." They said they'd wait a little longer, in case we were wrong and Nell and the rest of them came back, after all.

The pine needles covered the woods floor in a thick layer. They were slippery and smelled wonderful. When I was little, I had a pillow filled with pine needles that I used to sleep on until some of them worked their way through the covering and poked me in the face. I still have that pillow somewhere. I walked way back into the woods until I found the little wooden cross we'd been told by old timers marked the graves of three Indians buried there. Some said the cross was nothing but the marker for the grave of an old tabby cat, but I didn't believe that. A crow cawed somewhere above me, and another crow answered. Patches of leftover snow lay tucked back in the deepest part of the wood, and the small brook we used to fish in was running high. Maybe me and the boys would fish there this spring when the smelts were running. We never caught anything, but it was always fun trying. The ground was spongy soft in places. Not soft enough to bury a dog in but almost.

I kept my eyes open. There were no traces of the old dog. It was as if he'd never been.

I never saw Nell again. As my father had guessed, they'd skipped town owing money, not only to Mr. Johnson but to lots of other people. They'd taken Rowena's mother's fur coat, the cigar box with our profits from the yard sale. The works.

It was as if Nell had never been, either. I kept thinking she might send me a postcard from wherever it was they'd gone to from here. But I never heard from her. After a while a new family moved into the house. They had two little boys just the right ages for Tad and Sidney. I dream about Nell now and then. She flashes her green fingernails and whispers about making their tongues tingle. I refuse to be sorry for her. I absolutely refuse.

I told my mother about her. About how she said her hair was naturally curly, about her brothers and how they'd been in practically every state in the union, except for some of the M's and Alaska and Hawaii. About Uncle Joe and her other uncle with the spread out West and fifty horses. Maybe that's where they were headed right at this minute. About her father who'd flown the coop. And how she didn't want me to show her where the principal's office was on her first day of school. About her not wearing any underpants if she didn't feel like it.

"She sounds like somebody you'll always remember, that's for sure," my mother said.

She's right. I will.

You have to know how to separate the wheat from the chaff, my father says. You have to learn to pick and choose. Life is full of decisions and surprises. And disappointments.

I'm sadder and wiser than I was before Nell moved up the road from us. I'm also not as mean as I once was.

Ask anybody.

I said to Rowena, "Have you noticed I'm not as mean as I once was?" All she said was, "That's what you think."

What does she know.

Constance Greene

One author who makes
kids *laugh at themselves*—
when growing up gets them down.